Stealing the Duke's Heart

Featuring *How to Steal a Duke* and

Taken by the Duke

Shana Galen

Acknowledgments

Thank you to all the readers who email me with compliments and criticism, ideas, and recommendations, and who always have suggestions when I need help with a title or cover or plot point. I very much appreciate two fabulous readers who suggested the title of this duet. Thank you, Denise Holcomb and Molly Moody!

How to Steal a Duke

(in Ten Days, Give or Take a Few Days, But Definitely in Less than a Fortnight)

Chapter One

"What do you mean you don't have it?" Dominick Spencer, the Duke of Tremayne, slammed his fist on the desk, rattling the tea cup perched on its delicate blue and white china saucer.

"I'm s-sorry, Your Grace," the agent stammered, shrinking back as though he wished he could blend into the wood paneling of the duke's London town house. "I have exhausted every avenue—"

"Damn and blast your *every avenue*." Dominick stood and stalked around the large oak desk that had been his father's and his grandfather's and his great-grandfather's before that. "You didn't exhaust every avenue, or you'd have the book in your hands by now."

"Yes, Your Grace." The man hung his head, staring down at the hat he had crumpled in his hand. "I will keep trying—"

Dominick waved an arm. "Get out."

The agent looked up quickly.

"Get out of my library and my house, and while you're at it, get out of my employ. Mr. Jones, you are relieved of your position."

"It's Jarvis, Your Grace."

Dominick took two more menacing steps. He was a large man, three or four inches over six feet, with brawn he had cultivated from fencing, pugilism, and riding. He did not drink spirits. He did not gamble. He did not socialize.

He had a half-dozen estates to oversee and thousands of tenants, servants, and others relying on him. The Duke of Tremayne was one of the most powerful men in England, and he ruled his dominion with an iron fist. Either an employee did as he or she was hired to do, or he was out.

Dominick glared down at the agent. "I don't bloody care what your name is. You are through." He pointed to the door, and Jones or Jarvis or whoever the hell he was scurried out.

As soon as the agent was gone, Quincey entered. The secretary was a man of about sixty, of average height and build, with white hair and small, round spectacles. He knew not to speak until addressed, and so he waited patiently while Dominick leafed through several papers on his desk. They were in a neat stack precisely in the center of the desk and arranged alphabetically. He found the one he wanted easily and removed it, straightening the stack again before turning to his secretary.

"Tell Fitch I want my hat and coat."

"Yes, Your Grace. Shall I inform the butler you will not be dining at home? He will want to notify Cook."

Dominick waved a hand without looking up from the paper. "Fine." He didn't care about food. He cared about the book. He and two other members of the Bibliomania Club had pledged to find the four volumes of a manuscript known as *The Duke's Book of Knowledge*. Dominick didn't need another book. He had a library full of rare and extraordinary books, as did the other members of the club. They were all collectors, usually in competition for the ancient volumes. But this was not about his own library. Not this time. This was about Professor Peebles, who had been his instructor at Oxford. Peebles's literature class had inspired Dominick's love of rare and unusual books. And for as long as Dominick had known the professor, he'd been searching for *The Duke's Book*.

Now Peebles was an old man and ready to retire, his one regret that he had never found any of the volumes of *The Duke's Book*. Four members of the Bibliomania Club, three of whom had been Peebles's students at Oxford, had each agreed to find one of the four volumes, and they planned to present them all to Peebles on the eve of his retirement. Even now, Viscount Daunt or the Earl of Ramsdale might have a volume of the manuscript in hand. Dominick had nothing, and the professor would retire in a little more than a fortnight.

Unacceptable.

"Is there anything else, Your Grace?" Quincey asked.

"Yes." Dominick folded the paper neatly and slid it into his pocket. "Make a note that I have fired Mr. Jarvis."

"Yes, Your Grace." Quincey's lined face betrayed no emotion. "I assume Mr. Jarvis did not manage to find the volume."

"He did not. It appears if I want something done, Quincey, I will have to do it myself."

"Your Grace?" Now Quincey's brows rose, and he managed to look both composed and slightly alarmed.

"That's right, Quincey. Jarvis is the third man I've hired, and not a one of them has found the volume. I don't have any time left to waste. Have Bateman pack me a valise. Tomorrow I leave to find the volume on my own."

Once at the club, Dominick climbed the wide stairs to the second floor, which housed a drawing room, where the members often met to discuss their acquisitions, and an extensive library, full of books about... well, books. This was the room members visited if they wanted to research a particular book to ascertain its value. Some books were valuable because of their content. Others were exceedingly rare. Still others were not so rare, but were volumes any bibliophile worth his salt would have in his collection.

Dominick opened the door to the research library and inhaled the smell of leather, ink, and old parchment paper. It was an intoxicating scent. The room was dark, as no fire or sconces were allowed inside, and Dominick took a lamp from the table just outside the doorway, lit it, and stepped inside, closing the door after him. He set the lamp on the polished oak table in the center of the room and strode to the medieval section of the library.

The Duke's Book of Knowledge had been commissioned by Lorenzo de' Medici in the fifteenth century. The volume Dominick sought was filled with arcane medical knowledge. He had consulted experts in the field, but thus far, all of their suggestions as to where the medical volume had been hidden had proved fruitless.

He pulled a book off the shelf, one he had perused many times, and read silently under a section titled *The Duke's Book of Knowledge*.

... secretly commissioned book of knowledge to be assembled from the greatest scholarship, written in a fine Italic hand by a team of Florentine scribes, and illustrated by great artists. Very few eye-witness descriptions of the book exist.

Dominick skipped ahead. He didn't care where the eye-witness descriptions might be chronicled. He knew those descriptions from memory at any rate. There were four bound volumes, each with a Roman numeral on the spine. His finger slid down the page.

... in the possession of François I of France, Philip II of Spain and, finally, the Duke of Buckingham, James I's favorite, who was said to have brought the volumes to England. After the Duke was assassinated in 1628, the manuscript disappeared from view...

Dominick knew all of this. He replaced the tome and pulled down another. This one stated that the Villiers family, Buckingham's surname, did not possess the manuscript upon the duke's death. The scholarly author suggested the four volumes had been dispersed.

"Oh, I beg your pardon, Your Grace. I did not mean to intrude. Just making my rounds."

Dominick glanced over his shoulder at the elderly man in the doorway. "You are not intruding, Mr. Rummage. In fact, I am just about through here."

Rummage, who served as the club's Master of the House, had been in that position ever since Dominick had joined. It was impossible to tell how old the man might be. He could have been sixty or eighty. His hair was gray and rather unruly, sticking up at all angles. His beard was just as bushy, but his watery eyes were sharp and keen. He was a tall, thin man, who dressed in black and who seemed to wander but always managed to be where he was needed. "Did you find what you were looking for, Your Grace?"

"Not exactly."

"Might I be of assistance?"

Dominick almost shook his head, then reconsidered. Rummage had been here a long, long time. Mightn't he have overheard a conversation or perhaps read a passage in one of these books that could be useful to Dominick?

"What do you know about *The Duke's Book of Knowledge?*" Dominick asked.

"Professor Peebles's manuscript?" Rummage stepped inside the room and closed the door behind him. "I know there are several of you searching for the volumes. You seek the medical volume, do you not, Your Grace?"

"I do, and I'm having a devil of a time finding it."

"I can well imagine, Your Grace. That's the one—well, I doubt I can be of use."

But Dominick had seen the hint of something in Rummage's eyes—a memory that caused a flicker of a smile and a slight crease in the older man's brow.

"I would not be so quick to dismiss you," Dominick said. "Come. Sit with me a moment and tell me, do you recall ever hearing anyone speak about *The Duke's Book*, specifically about the volume on medical knowledge?" Dominick took a seat at the oak table, but Rummage remained standing.

"I don't think it would be proper for me to sit, Your Grace, but I will say that I remember many, many conversations about *The Duke's Book*. The professor used to speak about it at length."

"Yes. I've consulted him, and I've had every location on his list searched to no avail. There must be somewhere else." He resisted the urge to scrub his hand over his tight jaw, which he assumed was darkening with stubble by this hour of the night.

"Then it wasn't in that old keep on the Cornwall coast?"

Very deliberately, Dominick straightened. "Cornwall, you say?"

"Yes. The Temples. To hear the professor talk about it, it sounded like a setting from one of the Gothic novels the ladies like to read. It always seemed more like a myth than a possible location for *The Duke's Book*."

Myth or not, Cornwall was not one of the locations Dominick had searched.

"But you did search The Temples, Your Grace?"

"No, Mr. Rummage, I have not. And now, I insist you sit right here and tell me all about it." He held up a hand. "Do not argue. I will call for tea, and we shall take our time going back over the conversation as best you recall it."

"Yes, Your Grace." Rummage sat, and Dominick went to the bell-pull to summon a servant.

The Temples. This was it. He could feel it, the same way he knew when a horse was of the best stock or an investment was sound. Dominick believed heartily in books and documents and research, but there was something to be said for instinct as well. The Dukes of Tremayne had been famous for their instincts for centuries. Instinct was how they'd known who among their vassals were traitors, which side of the War of the Roses to fight on, and which women to take to wife to ensure the bloodline.

Dominick trusted his instincts, which meant The Temples was where he would find that lost volume.

***

Miss Rosalyn Dashner had been called a cat more than once in her life. She'd first climbed out of her crib at the tender age of ten months, whereupon she then proceeded to crawl across the room and claw her way onto her toy box to retrieve the doll she wanted. Her nanny had returned to the nursery to find her charge scaling the railing to return to her crib.

And this was before Rosalyn could even walk.

As she grew older, she climbed bookshelves, trees, and even a trellis or two. But by the time she was fifteen, she was no longer climbing for fun. Her father had died, leaving her mother and her three siblings in dire straits indeed. Then Rosalyn's youngest brother, Michael, had become ill. The cost of doctors and medicines had been exorbitant. The once genteel family had fallen deeper and deeper into debt. They'd had to sell their small country house and move to the unfashionable Cheapside area of Town.

Rosalyn did not mourn the move. She adored London. London was alive. It reminded her of an enormous beehive that had hung from a tree on the path she liked to walk back in country. When she'd been five or six, she barely noticed it. But by the time she was twelve, the hive was so large it bent the branch on which it hung. Rosalyn had worried that a stiff breeze would send it tumbling to the ground, angry bees swarming about.

That was London. Year after year, it seemed to grow and expand until it became so dense and so large the mass of people within could barely be contained. And just like that beehive back home, London buzzed and hummed with constant activity. Rosalyn never felt alone in London. There was always someone awake and about, and usually their intentions were as dishonorable as her own. But now that summer was upon them and with it warmer days, tempers were shorter and foreheads damper. It seemed everyone was on edge, waiting for that stiff breeze that would dislodge the hive and catapult the city into violence.

Rosalyn had seen it before—brawls that turned into riots, riots that created mobs. London was woefully unprepared for such lawlessness. There was no centralized police force, and the watchmen snoozed more than they patrolled. Rosalyn had long thought she was fortunate to be a cat. Cats could tiptoe away when violence erupted, looking down on it all from the safety of a high branch.

Her branch tonight was the roof of Thomas & Sons on Canterbury Lane. Her older brother, Stephen, was beside her, lying on his back and smoking a cheroot, the smell of which reminded Rosalyn of her father's pipe. Stephen was more of a raven than a cat. He had sharp eyes and could pick a lock as though he'd been born to it. With his light brown eyes and dark black hair, he perched in shadows and moved through alleys so quickly it seemed he flew.

Daniel, on the other hand, could neither slink nor fly. He was a year younger than Rosalyn, and the two were often mistaken for twins. They both had dark hair, like Stephen, but their eyes were green, not brown. Rosalyn was shorter than Daniel, but Daniel was shorter than Stephen. Daniel and Rosalyn were both thin and wraithlike. Rosalyn used her small body to advantage, slipping into spaces most adults could not manage and hanging on pipes or clotheslines that would have bent or broken if someone with more weight had relied on them.

But for all the grace she had been given, Daniel had only awkwardness. He was gangly and clumsy, forever knocking over small tables and breaking Mama's few remaining china plates. For this reason, Daniel served as lookout, loitering below the shop, ready to signal when the shop owners had finished locking up for the night or if the watch happened by.

"It shouldn't be long now," Stephen said, blowing smoke into a sky already gray from coal fires.

"Not long," she agreed, peering over the edge of the building to keep her eye on Daniel. He slouched against a shop across the street, hands in his pockets, looking half asleep. But she caught the glint of his green eyes under the brim of his hat. He was alert and ready.

"You know what you're after?"

She glanced at Stephen, annoyed to find his dark eyes fixed on her.

"If you mean, do I remember how all of you voted against me, the answer is yes. I lost. No jeweled cameo. Instead, I'm to swipe a simple silver chain." Even she could hear the bitterness in her voice.

"We can sell the chain easily. Any of the popshops will take it. They can turn around and sell it again the next day. Who do we know that will have the blunt or the customers to pay for a jeweled cameo?"

Rosalyn had heard this tedious argument before. Stephen was probably just as tired of her response. "Then we find a buyer for the cameo. Or, forget the cameo. When I cased the shop last week, I saw rings and brooches. I could swipe one of those. We find the right buyer, and we're done thieving for a year or more."

Stephen raised a brow at her. "And here I thought you liked thieving."

She did like it. "That's not the point. Mama does not approve, and she's probably right. No matter how good we are, eventually we will be caught."

"You mean Danny or I will be caught. It would take another cat to catch you, Ros." He tousled her hair, which she'd pulled back into a long tail and tucked under her coat. She wore men's clothing because it was easier to move in. She'd often thought she should chop her hair off so she would not have to worry about it getting in the way or spoiling her disguise, but her hair was the only womanly thing about her. She was otherwise as thin and straight as a boy.

"I don't like to worry about you and Danny, but I also miss having some security. Having a little money would buy us security."

"And taking something that valuable would hurt the shop owners. They'll hardly miss a silver chain, but a ring worth thirty pounds might mean they go out of business. I hardly want to get rich by stepping on the backs of others trying to earn an honest living."

Rosalyn sighed. How could she argue with that? She had always been inclined to take the every-man-for-himself view. But she had gone in the shop, and the older gentleman who had offered assistance had been very kind. She didn't want to see him unable to pay his rent or feed his family.

"Fine." She peered over the roof again and then ducked back just as quickly. Danny was consulting his London guidebook, which was her signal that the owners were about to depart. "He has the guidebook," she whispered to Stephen.

Stephen stubbed out the cheroot and rolled onto his belly. Both of them listened intently to the street noise below. Gradually, she heard the jingle of bells as the door to the shop opened. The passing carriages and general hum of the hive that was London kept her from hearing the actual clicks of the keys in the locks, but she could imagine the sound. Then, after at least ten minutes had passed, she rose up on her elbows and peered over the roof again.

Daniel had put his guidebook away and was setting his pocket watch. She and Stephen knew the watch did not actually work, but it was a convenient signal.

The shop owners had departed.

"Still too light," Stephen said.

"I hate these long summer days," she replied. She'd loved them when she'd been young and carefree in the country. She'd been able to go for long walks after dinner down to the pond or the stables. But now that life had ended, long summer days meant waiting for the sun to creep low enough that she could melt into the shadows. And so much for dinner. Her mother would have some broth waiting for them when they returned. Perhaps bread as well. But it would barely quell the rumbling in her belly. And if she was hungry, she could only imagine how much worse it must be for Stephen, who was bigger and taller than she.

But the sacrifice was worth it for Michael. Sweet little Michael, who had been so ill and whose medicines and tonics and doctor's calls were so very expensive. Michael was fourteen now, but he looked much closer to the age of nine. He was so small and so pale. Rosalyn would have given her brother all of her dinner if it would have made any difference.

But nothing seemed to help. She did not like to admit it, but her brother was growing worse, not better. Rosalyn did not like to imagine life without Michael.

"Ros, it's time."

Shaken out of her dour thoughts by Stephen's voice, Rosalyn peered over the edge of the building and looked down. Indeed, the streets were gray and shadowed. She could barely discern the glow of Danny's cheroot.

She looked at Stephen. "Pull out the rope."

Chapter Two

"Tell me about The Temples," Dominick said, leaning over the hot cup of tea he did not want. Rummage had added cream and sugar to his, and Dominick judged he'd waited long enough for the information he wanted.

"I have never been myself, Your Grace," Rummage said, "but to hear the professor tell it, the place is more like a fortress than a home. It was a medieval keep at one time and had been heavily fortified at one time. It is located on the coast of Cornwall, high on the cliffs. It sounded a dark and treacherous place."

"Is it abandoned?"

"No. The professor went to The Temples and was refused entrance by the servants. It is said a mad earl lives there."

"Which earl?" Dominick knew his Debrett's, and he could think of no earl associated with a family estate called The Temples.

"Let me think. This conversation was at least a decade ago, perhaps more." Rummage sipped his tea, and Dominick refrained from tapping his fingers on the table.

"Ah, I have it. Verney. The Earl of Verney."

"Any idea how old this mad earl might be?" After all, if the professor had traveled to meet him a decade before, mightn't the earl be dead by now? Perhaps his much saner son held the property now, and if he needed blunt—and what noble with a crumbling cliffside structure did not need money?—might he be persuaded to sell the volume to Dominick?

"I couldn't say, Your Grace. Shall I consult Debrett's for you?"

"I can do it." Dominick rose to fetch the book, which was located near the door. "Tell me more about what you know of the professor's visit."

"He was turned away by the staff, and he always intended to go back. But he rather doubted the volume was located at The Temples, so he preferred to search elsewhere first. But I think he knew if the manuscript was lodged at The Temples, it was lost forever."

Dominick looked up from the page where he scanned the names of the peerage. "Why is that?"

"Not only was the earl mad and unreasonable, the structure itself was all but impregnable." Now Rummage lowered his voice. "I don't think it would surprise you, Your Grace, if I said the professor was not above actions some might consider rather shady to achieve his aims."

This did not surprise Dominick in the least.

"The professor said that one would have to be a monkey or a cat to scale the walls of that keep, and a surefooted cat at that, what with the wind buffeting you."

"Hmm." Dominick supposed he would have to do what he always did—order his way in. He was a duke. He outranked an earl. But using his power didn't always have the best results. He might have used charm—if he'd had any. But what if...his finger slid over the entry for Verney. He frowned.

Unless the earl had died in the last year or so, he was very much alive and very much ensconced, a recluse it seemed, in The Temples.

And that meant the volume was very much out of Dominick's reach.

***

Rosalyn lowered herself over the side of the building and took a moment to find purchase for her feet. She wore thin gloves that kept her hands warm but allowed them the freedom of movement. She'd changed from her boots into the sort of slippers a dancer or a tightrope walker might wear. These gave her toes a better grip.

She'd removed her coat and descended slowly in shirt-sleeves and trousers. Her fingers gripped the fine but sturdy rope Stephen had dropped down. Since they couldn't risk him standing on the street picking the lock of Thomas & Sons, she would descend to the window and enter on the shop's first floor. The family's residence was elsewhere, and though she did not know what the first floor might house, she knew from her observations that no one slept on the premises.

The rope was secured about her waist, but Rosalyn wrapped a length of it loosely around her hand and used it to begin her descent. She kept close to the brick of the building, staying small and tight lest anyone happen to look up or out from one of the other windows. She was dressed in all black, which helped her to blend in. Above her, she could hear Stephen huffing. Now that night had fallen, the heat had begun to dissipate, but it was still hot and strenuous work to support all seven or eight stone of her over the side of a building.

She lowered herself carefully, picking her way delicately across the landscape of the bricks until she found the safest. Finally, she reached the lone window on this side of the upper story. She inched down until she was even with the sill, then positioned herself on the narrow ledge, sideways so her shoulder and thigh pressed against the glass. Now she released the rope she held in her hands, but should she fall, she had the protection of the knot at her waist.

Not that she would fall. She never fell.

Still, she hoped Stephen hadn't become complacent. If he wasn't gripping the rope, this could be the one night she tumbled to the hard ground below.

Rosalyn took her time to catch her breath, listening for Danny's whistle. The whistle was the sign everything was clear. When she heard it, she took a deep breath and attempted to slide the window open.

It didn't budge.

She hadn't expected it to open easily, but there was no reason not to try. It was too dark for her to see whether the window was secured by some sort of lock, but given that it wasn't the ground floor, she doubted it. No reason to lock a window on the first floor, especially when one might wish to open it and allow air to circulate. But it was still early in the summer, and perhaps no one had needed to open it since last fall. The painted wood might be stuck to the casement at the sill.

She reached into her boot and unsheathed her knife. It had a long, thick blade. She had never used it as a weapon, but it was wonderful for prying open recalcitrant doors or windows. If her blade didn't work, she'd have to break the glass. But given that the glass was thick, breaking it was her last option.

Adjusting her position so she didn't slip backward, Rosalyn slid the blade between the sill and the window casement. The fit was tight, and it took some wriggling to wedge the blade all the way in. Keeping her balance under such conditions was a fine art of knowing just how to shift one's weight and when. Rosalyn gritted her teeth and pressed the blade up, trying to free the casement from the sill. This too was a tricky endeavor, because she did not want to break the blade. Finally, she felt the wood of the casement give, and she twisted the knife vertically, forcing space between the two pieces of wood.

She withdrew the knife and stuck it back in her boot, then tucked her small fingers into the space she'd created. It was a beastly tight fit, but she managed it, then pushed up with all her strength.

With a creak, the window lifted. She didn't need much space, and as soon as she had it, she slipped one leg inside, then the other. When she was standing inside the dark chamber, she grasped her knife again and cut the rope from her waist. There was no point in attempting to untie it. It would be knotted too tightly. She tugged on it twice to let Stephen know she was free of it, then left it dangling inside the half-open window. She'd need it on the way out.

Rosalyn surveyed the room she stood in. It was an open chamber, running the entire length of the small shop below. A table with chairs sat near the other window, which would receive the morning light. On the table were small instruments that she did not know the names of but that she associated with jewelry making. This was obviously the place where the family repaired broken jewelry as well as made the jewelry patrons requested.

There was also a large safe in the far corner, and it was closed and locked. This might have been a short night if someone had left a silver or gold chain lying out. But thieving had never been so convenient for her. She'd have to make her way downstairs and find a suitable piece. She had an idea of the one she wanted—not too showy but a good piece nonetheless.

She wove past a chest of drawers and a desk and padded silently over the carpet until she reached the steps. They had been designed in an L-shape, which meant she would go down about half a dozen, then have to turn on the landing and finish her descent. There was something about the landing she didn't care for, though. It was too…light. Had someone left a lamp burning? Was that where the light filtering up from the ground floor to the landing originated?

If the steps had been straight down, she would have been able to see what she was moving toward, but as it was, she was blind.

Daniel had definitely signaled that the shop owners had departed and locked the door. No one was here, so the light must have been a forgotten candle or lamp. Still, Rosalyn paused and waited for a long moment, listening. She heard nothing but the thud of horses' hooves a street over and a hawker attempting to sell pies.

She put her foot on the first step and slowly lowered her weight onto it. Then she did the same with the other. Her progress was slow, but she could not be too careful. Now was the time when she really must prowl. She'd descended four of the six steps to the landing and was just placing her foot on the fifth when she heard a slight cough. The sound startled her, and she would have pulled her foot up, but it was too late. Her body's momentum was forward, and she ended up lowering her foot harder than she would have liked.

The step creaked. Loudly.

"Who's there?" a man's voice called.

Rosalyn froze.

***

Dominick looked up from the notes he'd taken of his conversation with Rummage and frowned. His carriage was not moving. How long had they been sitting still? He'd been reading by the light of the carriage lamps and hadn't really taken note when they'd stopped. He'd been so engrossed that they might have been sitting here for an age. Dominick parted the curtains, saw very little in the darkness outside, and rapped on the roof with his walking stick.

John Coachman opened the hatch. "Yes, Your Grace?"

"Why are we stopped?"

"Terribly sorry, Your Grace. There's a line of carriages on the way to Covent Garden."

Some play or other was doubtless debuting, and the *ton* wanted to be present. Not to watch the performance, but to be seen in attendance. Ridiculous. When Dominick attended a play, he went to see the play, not ogle the audience with opera glasses. "I am not attending the performance," he said.

"No, Your Grace," the coachman agreed.

"Then move us out of the line of conveyances."

"I would, Your Grace, but it would mean taking a more roundabout route home."

"I don't care. Just get us moving again." Dominick used the handle of his walking stick to slam the hatch closed. The carriage began, slowly, to move again, and Dominick tried to go back to his reading, but his focus had been interrupted. Instead, he parted the curtains and peered out.

There wasn't much to see—the usual carts full of coal or firewood, a flower girl attempting to sell her last few wilting daisies, and a few couples making their way, on foot, toward Covent Garden. None of which shed any light on his current dilemma. How the devil was he to gain access to the library in The Temples? If the mad earl was as much a recluse as everyone seemed to think, Dominick might push his way in, but how would he be able to confront the earl and persuade him to relinquish the manuscript? He certainly couldn't scale the crumbling walls and climb inside the earl's chamber. Rummage had laughed about needing a cat. Where was Dominick to find a cat?

Just then, something large and heavy thudded on the roof of his carriage. John Coachman called to the horses to stop, and Dominick stuck his head out. The sight that greeted him shocked him.

Then it made him smile.

***

"Who's there?" called the voice again.

Rosalyn pushed down a surge of panic. Someone was here! A man, by the sound of the voice, was still in the shop, and he'd heard her. Even now, he was listening for her to move again.

Rosalyn didn't have time to wonder how Daniel had made this mistake, or to think how they might find another way to acquire the blunt they needed for Michael's medicine. All she could think of was escape. And the one avenue of escape she had was the open window. She turned on her heel and raced back upstairs.

But she was well and truly caught now. She could hear the man coming after her, his hard-soled shoes thumping on the steps as he went up. Rosalyn was quick and nimble, but she didn't have time to secure the rope around her waist again. Nor did she want Stephen caught at the other end of it if she didn't manage to get away. She skidded to a stop before the window, grasped the rope and tugged it three times. That was the signal for Stephen to pull the rope up and fly away.

She'd never had to use this signal before, and there was a moment's hesitation before the rope started to rise. No doubt Stephen hadn't wanted to leave her, but he knew as well as anyone that she didn't need a rope to escape. Plus, as a woman, she would be treated with much more leniency than he or Daniel. She heard the whistle that alerted Daniel to run just as her pursuer stumbled into the upper chamber.

"I knew it!" he yelled in triumph. He was a young man, probably twenty or so, close to her own age. He had rusty hair and a profusion of freckles, visible in the light of the candle he held in one hand. A clerk, she thought. He'd stayed behind to do…whatever clerks did…and they hadn't accounted for him. The shop owners had locked the front door, but what if there was a back door they'd instructed the clerk to use when he'd finished for the night?

And why hadn't she considered this before she was standing in front of him?

He reached out a thin hand, pointing a long finger at her. "Thief! Watchman! Thief!"

Oh, blast it all. He was one of those. She'd hoped he might take her on himself. She could defend herself with a well-placed kick, but if he insisted on bringing all of London down on them, she had only one option—climb out the window.

Rosalyn ducked through the open window and immediately dropped down so her hands held on to the sill but her feet dangled freely below. She wouldn't bother trying to climb up. It was slow and difficult work. It would be much faster to use gravity to her advantage and climb down. Of course, she would need to do so quickly, before the watch did make an appearance.

She moved her feet, feeling for any sort of ledge or nook. When she found a small outcropping, she braced one foot on it and then trailed her other foot until she found another.

In the meantime, the clerk had stuck his head out the window and screamed for the watch.

The clerk's screaming bought her time to lower herself below the casement. Her arms shook when she released the sill, out of fatigue and fear. She was balanced on the thinnest of perches and would have to climb all the way to the ground this way. Since she'd been on only the first floor, she wouldn't have to climb far before she could drop down to the ground and run, but the descent was in no way easy.

She imagined from below it might look like she was clinging to the sheer brick wall, but what most people didn't realize was that almost every structure had irregularities, and one could use those as foot- and handholds if one was small and nimble.

She found another outcropping, big enough for most of her toes, and perched on it. One of her hands slipped, and she tried to ignore the panic that came with the possibility of falling. She found another place to put her hand, a bit flatter than she would have liked, and held on.

Thus, slowly, very slowly, she began to climb down. She was so intent upon her work that she didn't notice the clerk any longer. At least not until he hurled a book down at her. He missed, but not by much. She looked up and scowled. She hadn't even stolen anything, and he was trying to kill her?

A glance down told her she still had some ways to go before she could jump. She also saw the book land on the top of a passing carriage. The coachman paused, his mouth dropping open as he spotted her. Rosalyn went back to the task at hand. She couldn't hurry, much as she wanted to, and so forced herself to take her time finding the next outcropping and balancing on it before lowering herself another foot or so.

Another book sailed toward her, bouncing off her shoulder. She bit her lip to stifle the flinch of pain and maintained her tenuous hold.

"You there!" came an imperious voice. "Stop that at once!"

Rosalyn could not help but look down. There, emerging from the carriage that had halted, was a tall man dressed in dark breeches, a white shirt and cravat, and a dark coat. He looked up at her, his bright blue eyes peering out from under the shadow of his beaver hat. His eyes were striking, and he would have been handsome if his expression hadn't been so severe. Those turquoise eyes were hard, his lips a thin line, his jaw tight, his cheeks sharp slashes. Rosalyn had the urge to climb right back up again. She rather thought she might fare better with the book thrower than this man.

He was a noble. She didn't even have to look at the cut of his clothes or the shine of his carriage to know that. Everything about him spoke of nobility—and the imperiousness that came with it. She'd moved in those circles once, perhaps not such exalted circles as this man must occupy, but she was familiar with the look of privilege and hauteur.

"Watchman!" the clerk yelled above her. "Stop this thief!"

"I haven't stolen anything, you dolt!" Rosalyn yelled back. Her shoulder still stung from the impact of the last tome he'd thrown.

"You there!" the nobleman called. "Climb down here."

Rosalyn looked down at him, then back up at the clerk. She couldn't hang on forever. Her arms ached, and the muscles still shook with fatigue. Her toes were numb and would soon cramp from clinging to the small foothold.

"Lad, climb down," the nobleman ordered. "No harm will come to you."

As though she believed that, but she didn't have the strength left to climb back up, so down seemed the way to go. Besides, once the nob realized she was a woman, he might be more likely to give her clemency. Still taking care, she began to descend again. The clerk disappeared from the window above, and Rosalyn assumed he would be waiting on the street below when she landed on solid ground. Her hands had begun to cramp, and her arms and legs shook so badly with strain that she almost lost her grip. But she held on, descended another foot, then glanced down. The drop was not so far. She could make it.

Releasing the building's wall, she jumped, landing in a crouch. She stayed down, swiveling to face the nobleman and the clerk, who stood beside him. "Watch!" the clerk called.

"Stubble it," the nobleman ordered, coming toward her. Rosalyn might have shrunk back, but she had nowhere to go. Instead, she rose fluidly to her full height, quite a few inches shorter than he, and stared up at him defiantly.

"What is your name, boy?" he asked.

"They call me The Cat," she said.

His eyes widened with interest. "I can see why. You're not a boy either."

"And I'm not a thief." This was not completely true, but she hadn't stolen anything tonight. "I didn't take anything from that man." She nodded to the clerk. With some dismay, she noted a watchman was approaching, waddling as quickly as he could manage.

"Then what were you doing in the shop?" His gaze shifted to the sign above the door. "The jewelry shop, after it had been closed for the day?"

She met his gaze, feeling very much like a schoolgirl under the critical eye of her governess.

"What's this about?" the watch demanded. "What is happening here?"

"He's a thief!" the clerk said, pointing to her. "He picked the lock on the shop, and if I hadn't stopped him, he would have robbed Mr. Thomas blind."

"Is this true?" the watch asked her.

"No," she said. "He has it all wrong. I'm not a he. I'm a she. And I didn't pick any lock. Go ahead and check them if you don't believe me. I don't know the first thing about picking locks." That wasn't precisely true either.

"Then how was it you managed to be crawling out of the shop's window?" the nobleman asked.

"Now see here," the watch said, his face growing red with annoyance. "I am asking the questions, Mr.—"

One of the footmen who had been riding on the coach stepped forward. "You will address the duke as Your Grace."

The watchman's small eyes widened. "Duke? I'm terribly sorry, Your Grace. Do forgive me."

Duke. Wonderful. She had somehow managed to not only attract the notice of a clerk and the watch but also a duke. Her mother had always said one day she would be caught. This appeared to be the day.

"As I was saying," the duke continued, looking at her, "can you explain how you came to be crawling out of the shop's window?"

"Of course," she said with a decisive nod. "I fell into it by mistake. I was making my way to the ground floor to ask for assistance when this man"—she looked at the clerk—"began yelling and accusing me of theft. Naturally, I ran."

"Naturally."

She couldn't tell whether the duke believed her or not. His voice and expression betrayed nothing. The sky was darkening as night came upon the city, and she could barely make out his features.

"Did you hear that?" the clerk spluttered. "How did she fall into a closed window?"

"Are you certain it was closed?" the duke asked, never taking his gaze from her. The longer he looked at her, the warmer she felt.

"Well, no, but it's always closed."

"But you can't be certain," the duke said.

"I'd like to know how the chit fell." The watch waddled up to her, hands on his hips. "Do you claim you can fly, girl?"

"I like to walk on the roofs," she said. "It's much safer than the streets for a woman like me."

The three men stared at her, the watch and the clerk clearly incredulous. The duke's expression was still unreadable. Rosalyn blew out a breath of air. This was the end, then.

"That's the most ridic—" the clerk began.

"That makes perfect sense to me," the duke declared.

"It does?" The watchman's eyes bulged.

Rosalyn's own eyes felt like bulging as well. It was, as the clerk had no doubt been about to point out, a ridiculous story.

"Clearly, she isn't a thief," the duke declared. Rosalyn fumbled to turn out her pockets in illustration. The duke looked at the clerk. "Has anything been taken?"

"I-I don't know." The clerk eyed her empty pockets. "I would have to inventory everything."

"Do that, sir. In the meantime, I will escort this lady home. If you discover something has been stolen, appeal to my solicitor for compensation." He reached into his coat and handed the clerk a card. "If you will excuse us."

A footman opened the door to the carriage, and the duke gestured for her to climb inside. Rosalyn looked at the clerk, the watch, and then the duke. Her choice was clear. She could stay and go to prison, or enter the duke's carriage and… and she knew not what might happen. Prison or a duke's carriage… She took the footman's hand and climbed into the carriage.

This night had not ended at all as she'd planned, but one thing was clear. The duke had just rescued her.

The question was why.

Chapter Three

She was a small thing—petite was how his mother would have put it. But she wasn't a child. He'd seen the lift of her chin and the flash of determination in her green eyes. No, she was a woman, and an intelligent one at that.

She was also a thief. When he'd seen her scaling the wall of the shop, he'd known exactly what she'd been about. She probably deserved to be left to the mercy of the watch and whatever magistrate she was brought before.

Except Dominick needed someone who could scale walls, and this woman was a veritable cat.

"What's your name?" he asked as he settled back in his seat across from her.

"The Cat."

"Your real name."

She blinked at him, her eyes large in the dim light from the carriage lamps and her lips clamped shut.

"Very well. Where do you live?"

"Here and there."

He crossed his arms. "I fear my coachman needs more specific directions than that."

"Then you do intend to take me home?" She sounded surprised, as well she might. She had no idea what he meant to do with her. And she probably wouldn't like it when she found out.

"Of course."

"There's no need, Your Grace. I can make it on my own."

Oh, now she was referring to him as *Your Grace*. He smiled thinly. "I wouldn't want you to risk your welfare on the dangerous streets or chance... falling into any more open windows."

"No risk of that, Your Grace. My mother and brothers are waiting for me, so I'll just be off." She reached for the door, and he closed his gloved hand over hers.

"I said I would take you home, and that is what I plan to do. Now, Miss... Cat. We can sit here all night, or you can tell me where you live and we can be on our way. I prefer the latter."

"I prefer none of the above. Unhand me, please."

He ignored her. "I wonder at your identity, Miss Cat. Your accent is that of an educated person, and correct me if I'm mistaken, but you are not from London."

"You are not mistaken."

"I never am."

She rolled her eyes at that remark. He was almost offended. He could not remember the last time anyone had dared roll their eyes at him. Perhaps one of his siblings had when they'd been in the nursery.

"Then might I assume that you were intent upon stealing from that jewelry shop—no, I do not believe your absurd claim to have fallen into the window—because your family has fallen on hard times?"

She said nothing, but her expression was full of suspicion. She might not have been raised in London, but she knew enough to be wary.

"You mentioned a mother and brothers, but you did not mention a father." He knew this story well. A woman was widowed and then taken advantage of by unscrupulous sorts. Soon, she was destitute and forced to move to London to find honest work and cheap housing. Neither were to be readily found, and the widow was forced to take on less-honest work. In this case, it appeared her children had gone that route.

Dominick would help them. Not because he cared, although it couldn't be said he didn't care—he gave to various charitable organizations—but because aiding her would serve his purposes.

"I have a proposition for you, one that will ensure neither you nor your family want for funds in the near future."

She stiffened. The hand that had lain docilely beneath his jerked away. "You mistake me, Your Grace. I am no doxy you can buy for a night."

He stared at her, at this thin, small woman dressed in men's clothing. She was about the furthest thing from the sort of woman he'd want in his bed as he could imagine.

"Now open this door, or I shall scream until someone comes to rescue me."

He leaned forward. "First of all, no one will come to your aid no matter how much you scream. I am the Duke of Tremayne. I have more money than, if not God, certainly the king. You leave when I say you leave."

She opened her mouth to protest, but he held up a hand.

"Secondly, *you* mistake *me*, Miss Cat. I do not want your body. You hold absolutely no appeal for me. I want to buy your skills as a thief. I have a... job, so to speak, and I need someone with your abilities. You acquire the object I need, and I pay you. We part ways and never need meet again."

She stared at him for a very long time, so long, in fact, that he realized he'd been disingenuous, inadvertently, when he'd said she held no appeal for him. Her eyes were really quite beautiful, and her skin looked far softer than it should have, considering her "profession." Then there was her mouth, plump and red—

"I accept."

He snatched his gaze from her lips. "I beg your pardon?"

"I said, I accept."

"Of course you do." He sat back smugly, ignoring her eye roll. Two in the space of a quarter hour. The next dozen days would be a trial indeed.

"Where is this object?" she asked.

"I will tell you more as you need to know. Suffice it to say, the object I seek is not in London. You and I will have to travel to reach its location."

She bit her lip, seeming to consider this. He watched the way her small white teeth seemed to sink into the lush flesh.

"I need half the fee up front, then."

"I see." He'd been expecting this. "What is your fee, might I ask?"

"It's hard to say since you won't give me any details."

"Shall we say fifty pounds?"

Her mouth dropped open. It was almost comical the way she gaped at him. He hadn't been this amused in a very long time.

But she closed her mouth and narrowed her eyes. "If you are willing to give me fifty pounds, what you have planned must be dangerous."

"It could be, but from what I have seen, it will be nothing you cannot handle. Do hurry up and make your decision. I plan to leave first thing in the morning, and there are arrangements yet to be made."

She gulped, like a fish struggling to breathe out of water. "I said I accept, and I do. Give me the twenty-five pounds now, and I will meet you at your town house at first light. Where do you live?"

"I don't think so, Miss Cat. Once I pay you, you are mine. I don't allow you out of my sight. That's a protection on my investment."

"I cannot simply disappear. My family will be frantic with worry."

"Which brings us right back to where we began. Where do you live? I will take you home, you may collect what you need, say your farewells, and we will be off."

"And you will give my mother the money, the twenty-five pounds?"

"I will press it into her hand personally."

She closed her eyes tightly, reminding him of someone about to leap off a very tall cliff. When she opened them again, he saw that determined glint again. "My name is Rosalyn Dashner. If you summon your coachman, I'll give him my address."

***

This was a mistake. This had to be a mistake. Why on earth had she agreed to this ludicrous plan? Her mother and brothers would never agree to it. She couldn't run off to God knew where with a duke. But as the carriage sped closer and closer to the small flat her family rented, and the moment approached when she would have to explain to her mother and brothers the bargain she had struck, Rosalyn couldn't summon the will to tell the duke she'd changed her mind.

She *hadn't* changed her mind. This was their chance to break the chains of poverty that had been taking an ever firmer hold. With fifty pounds, they could pay the doctor's fees, the rent, and buy food and coal to see them through the winter. The little her mother earned from sewing could be put aside for the future, and her brothers could look for work instead of spending all day plotting burglaries with her and all night carrying them out.

And she could... Well, she could finally be a help to her mother. She might nurse Michael or help with the sewing or even take in some washing. This fifty pounds would mean they could finally get ahead, instead of always struggling to catch up.

She glanced at the man seated across from her. He sat facing the rear, which was the less desirable seat. Even though he'd not known her father was a gentleman, he'd treated her as a lady. He probably wasn't aware she understood his show of regard. He stared out the curtains she had parted earlier, his face impassive. Now that he'd struck his bargain, he was silent. He was no fool, then. He wouldn't risk saying anything that might make her change her mind. And she had enough questions to fill a library. What did he want her to steal? Why did a duke even need to steal? And what would happen if she failed? Not that she planned to fail. But, of course, she hadn't planned to fail tonight.

"How did you come to be outside Thomas & Sons tonight?" she asked.

His eyes never left the window. "I told my coachman to take a different route to my town house. The streets around Covent Garden were crowded."

A new show was opening. She'd seen the pamphlets. "But how did you know I would be there?" she asked. "Have you had me followed?"

His gaze touched on her briefly. "Our paths crossing was merely coincidence. Until the moment that book landed on the roof of my carriage, I had no idea you even existed."

She studied his face, which remained stoic. He didn't look as though he was lying. "Your Grace, I am a thief, and you need a thief. That seems a rather large coincidence."

He shrugged. "I didn't need a thief. I happened to see you, realized what you were, and decided I could use a thief. Perhaps I misspoke when I said our meeting was coincidence. I should have said it was an opportunity— one I think will be mutually beneficial."

He looked like a man who made use of opportunities. He was probably a man who had opportunities fall in his lap, so to speak, every day. At one time, she had felt like her life was charmed. Not any longer. Now it seemed anything could go wrong and usually did. "What if I fail?" she asked. She didn't want to bring up the possibility, but she had to know. He might ask the impossible of her. With his rigid posture, perfectly pressed clothing, and carefully chosen words, he looked like a man who had high expectations.

His eyes were not as bright blue in the glow of the carriage lamps, but his gaze was still intense when it rested on her. "You won't." It was an order.

"I appreciate your faith in my abilities, but I like all my threads knotted. If I fail, does my mother have to give back the twenty-five pounds?"

He leaned forward. "Miss Dashner, if you fail, you will have much larger worries than what happens to the twenty-five pounds." The carriage slowed to a stop. "Ah, we are here."

***

John Coachman opened the door, and Dominick stepped out into a street full of shops that were closed for the night. He didn't recognize it, but the address she had given was in Cheapside. He supposed her living situation might have been worse. This wasn't Seven Dials, with its gangs of pickpockets on the streets and prostitutes on the corners. But the shops here were shabby, the street muddy and in disrepair, and the gin shop just opposite them seemed to be doing a brisk business.

Miss Dashner climbed out. It was difficult to think of her as a *miss* in her men's clothing, especially when he'd seen her dangling on the side of a building, but in his travels around the world, he'd seen stranger things. "Lead on, Miss Dashner," he said.

She gave him an alarmed look. She seemed to have a large store of them, and she chose one to toss to him every few minutes. They were mostly similar in that her mouth dropped open or her eyes widened or she blinked at him with horror. This time, her brow furrowed, and she stepped back. "You needn't come in, Your Grace. I live just above that shop there. I'll go speak to my mother and return in a quarter of an hour."

He had no doubt she could be halfway across London in a quarter of an hour. "I told you that from now on you do not leave my sight."

She frowned, that supple mouth turning down at the corners. "But surely you cannot watch me every single moment. I must have privacy to sleep or attend to personal needs." She flushed at the last, reminding him very much of many of the young ladies he met in Society.

"If I am not able to be with you, someone else will be. But at the moment, there is no one acceptable save me. So lead on."

"But—"

"Miss Dashner, I tire of arguing each and every point with you. It grows irksome. Kindly follow my orders the first time I give them, and we will waste far less time."

Her eyes flashed emerald fire, which was a nice change from her expressions of alarm. He would have called her appearance one of outrage. It interested him, as most people didn't have the backbone to show him any outrage, but her look didn't faze him.

Hands on her hips, she leaned close. "Your Grace." She practically spat the courtesy. "If you think I will follow your orders like one of your servants, think again. You may pay me for one job, but I don't work for you."

He watched her lips move, those red full lips, and hardly listened to her words. Finally, she stopped speaking, and he had to pause to think about what she'd said. He obviously took longer than was customary, because she prodded, "Did you hear me?"

"I heard you," he said.

"And?"

And he had no intention of bowing to her demands. He was the Duke of Tremayne. His way was the only way.

Except he needed that damn volume, and he wasn't at all confident he could acquire it without her special skills. It was a rare thing for him to need anyone, and he was not quite certain what to do about it. His instinct was to walk away that moment. She could go her way, and he'd go his. But he fought against that instinct. "I hired you, and I give the orders. That much should be obvious. Now, shall we stand about in the cold, or shall we collect your belongings, say your good-byes, and be on the way?"

He saw the struggle in her face—the way she pressed her lips together—and her body—the way she clenched her hands into fists. She needed him every bit as much as he needed her. "I propose a compromise," she said, though her voice sounded strained, and she spoke through teeth locked together.

"I am a duke. I don't compromise."

"Then I walk away." She spoke confidently and without hesitation. He knew she'd do it.

"I'm listening," he said.

"I will take your orders into consideration on all matters up and until the actual"—she glanced at the coachman, who appeared very interested in the horses—"job. Then I take over as general."

"You don't even know the details."

"I know you've never so much as picked a pocket. You have your areas of expertise. I have mine." She stuck out her hand. She'd removed her gloves, and he stared down at her long, slim fingers. Did she want him to kiss her knuckles?

"Shall we shake on it?"

He almost chuckled. Shake on a deal with a woman? This was certainly proving to be an interesting evening. But he stuck out his hand and took her small one into his. "Now will you lead the way?"

She sighed. "Yes."

A few moments later, he saw why she had been hesitant to show him her home. It wasn't any shabbier than he'd expected. Though he was a duke, he had spent his share of time engaged in charitable endeavors or sitting with tenants in their simple cottages. And Dominick had spent enough time in London to know how the poor lived. Miss Dashner lived better than many. Still, it was a shock to duck his head and enter the small room crammed full of people. At least it seemed so. As soon as Miss Dashner opened the door, her mother was there, then her brothers. Upon seeing him, their questions ceased and they moved back as Miss Dashner led him inside. There was barely enough room for he and Miss Dashner to fit in the room, full as it was with the mother and her two brothers—three brothers, actually, he noted when he saw the young boy on a pallet in the far corner.

He scanned the room quickly, taking in the cold fireplace, the clothing hanging on lines from one side of the room to the other, and the furnishings, which he could see had once been lovely. Everything was clean, but the place had the lingering odor of potatoes and onions he always associated with the poor.

All eyes flew from him to Miss Dashner, and she held up a hand before what he assumed would probably be an onslaught of questions. Miss Dashner indicated the woman he assumed was her mother. "Mother, may I present the Duke of Tremayne. Your Grace, Mrs. Dashner."

Dominick was surprised the thief knew the proper form of introductions and then even more surprised when her mother dipped into a well-practiced curtsey. He nodded. "Ma'am."

"Your Grace," she said in the unmistakable accent of the upper class. His brows rose. "Might I introduce my sons, Mr. Stephen Dashner"—she pointed to a man who looked about five and twenty—"Mr. Daniel Dashner"—this one was younger and might have been the daughter's twin—"and Mr. Michael Dashner." He was the one on the pallet. He had the dark hair of the rest of the family, but he was very pale and scrawny.

"Your Grace," he said, his voice thin and reedy. "Forgive me if I do not rise."

"Pray, do remain seated, Mr. Dashner," Dominick replied. The boy was obviously ill. And what was even more obvious was that this family was not what he had expected at all. He should have expected it. The signs had been there—in the way Miss Dashner spoke and carried herself. But he'd been blinded by her masculine clothing and—truth be told—her very feminine lips.

"I see you have met my daughter," Mrs. Dashner said. "To what do we owe the honor of your presence?"

"His Grace saved me tonight," Miss Dashner said before Dominick could answer.

"How kind of the duke," Stephen Dashner said. "Mama, I told you, we were separated on our way home."

Mrs. Dashner sighed. Clearly, she did not believe her son. And the fact that the man saw the need to lie to his mother about his sister's—and possibly his own—illicit activities solidified Dominick's theory. This was a noble family who had fallen on hard times. As there was no father present, the mother had probably done the best that she could with what meager money she had. But the sick child had drained their provisions quickly, and the other children had turned to thieving, an occupation of which their mother did not approve.

"Stephen, it's no use," Miss Dashner said, then turned to her mother. "We were out attempting to pilfer a shop."

"Rosalyn!" Her mother inhaled sharply.

"I'm sorry, Mama, but that is the truth. It went badly, and in the course of my escape, I encountered the duke. If not for his intervention, I would be in the hands of the watch at this moment."

Mrs. Dashner clutched the white apron keeping her dress clean. "Then we owe His Grace our gratitude. May we offer you tea?"

"No, thank you, ma'am." If they had tea, he would certainly never dream of taking any for himself.

"He has no time for tea, Mama," Miss Dashner went on. "The duke saw my—er, unique skills and offered me a position."

The mother's hands stilled, and she went very rigid. "What sort of position?"

"I've asked her to assist me in acquiring an object I've been seeking," Dominick said. He had allowed Miss Dashner to tell her family the first part as she saw fit, but he could speak for himself. "The object is quite valuable, and I may have need of someone who can, shall we say, access difficult places."

"And you agreed to this?" Mrs. Dashner said, looking at her daughter.

"He will pay me fifty pounds."

Mrs. Dashner put a hand to her heart. "No. Absolutely not. This sounds not only illegal but also dangerous."

"I assure you it is not illegal." Dominick didn't intend for Miss Dashner to steal the volume. He would need her only if he could not gain access to the earl, in which case he'd have her—what had she said happened at the jewelry store?—*fall* into The Temples and persuade the earl to grant him an audience.

Perhaps the plan was slightly illegal.

"It might be mildly dangerous," he admitted, "but no less so than the activities your daughter was engaged in earlier tonight."

"But fifty pounds!" her mother said, backing toward one of the chairs and lowering herself slowly into it. "That is a great deal of money."

"The object is not in London. I will need Miss Dashner to travel with me for several days."

Mrs. Dashner's hand dropped from her heart. "I see."

"I will, of course, provide a chaperone. I will have one of my maidservants travel with us."

Miss Dashner glanced at him, clearly interested in the information he gave.

"She will be safe, or as safe as I can make her. Now, I don't mean to rush you, but time is of the essence. Miss Dashner, if you could collect your things?"

"Of course," she said. "But don't you have something for my mother first?"

He gave her an incomprehensible look and then remembered he'd promised payment up front. He took out his card. "Do you have a pen?" he asked. The Dashner who looked like the thief's twin indicated a quill and inkpot on a small table on the other side of the room. Dominick crossed to it in three strides, bent, and scrawled his vowels and twenty-five pounds on the back along with the name of his solicitor. "This is half the fee," he said, turning to give the card to Mrs. Dashner. "Take it to my solicitor, and he will give you the blunt."

Miss Dashner shook her head. "You said you would put it in her hands."

He gave her mother the card. "It is in her hands. I do not have that much on me."

"Surely this card will satisfy," Mrs. Dashner said, "but I don't like the idea of you leaving."

"I know, Mama. Come with me, and we will discuss it while I pack. Excuse me."

Finally, Miss Dashner went to gather her things. There was apparently another room, because she disappeared through a door. He could hear her voice and that of her mother's, though they spoke low enough that he could not make out the words. Dominick felt the gazes of Miss Dashner's three brothers and wished she would hurry.

"If you need a thief," Stephen Dashner said, "why not take me? I can pick locks, and I have the eyesight of a hawk."

Dominick shook his head. "I don't need locks picked or good eyes. I need someone who can climb." He glanced at Daniel Dashner. Perhaps he had his sister's skills, but Dominick didn't want to find out. He'd made his decision. He wanted Rosalyn Dashner. "I have already hired Miss Dashner, and she has agreed."

"You will understand if we are concerned," Daniel said. "She is our sister, and I'm afraid we do not know you very well, Your Grace."

"I understand completely, and I assure you your sister is perfectly safe with me."

"This is my fault," came a weak voice. They all turned their attention to the boy on the pallet. "It's because of me she has to go."

"Michael, no. This isn't your fault," Stephen Dashner said, going to his brother.

"Yes, it is. The doctor and the medicines cost too much. I begged Mama to simply let me die, then you would all be better off."

Dominick did not want to feel sympathy for the boy, but he felt his heart clench.

"Don't be a fool," Daniel Dashner said. "No one would be better off without you. And now we have enough money to pay for the doctor, the medicines, and more besides."

"But we lose Rosalyn."

Dominick cleared his throat. "Sir, I will bring her back." He didn't know how he could make that promise. After all, how could he prevent her from falling onto the rocky shoreline of Cornwall and smashing her head in? "You will see her in less than a fortnight," he said.

Michael Dashner looked at Dominick for a long, long time, his eyes large and dark. "Thank you," he said.

"If you don't mind my asking, what ails you?" Dominick asked. He had noted the bowl beside the couch and recognized it as the sort doctors often used to bleed patients. Personally, he didn't see the value in bleeding a person who was sick. It tended to weaken rather than strengthen him or her. Michael Dashner certainly looked weak.

"I have asthma."

"Which means?"

"I have trouble breathing. Sometimes I cannot catch my breath at all. I have always had difficulty, but—" He began to cough and wheeze.

Daniel Dashner moved forward and handed his brother a handkerchief, then poured liquid from one of the vials near the pallet into a cup and helped Michael Dashner swallow a bit.

"His condition worsened when we moved to London," Stephen Dashner finished. "The air isn't as clean here as it was in Surrey."

That was an understatement, Dominick thought. He moved closer to the table with the vials and peered at them. There must have been eight to ten. "What does that one do?" he asked Daniel Dashner as he capped it.

"It opens the lungs to allow more air inside."

Dominick sincerely doubted that. "Who is your doctor?"

"Doctor Banting. He's the best in the city," Daniel answered.

Dominick would see about that. A movement caught his eye, and he turned to see a pretty young woman walk out of the room where Miss Dashner and her mother had disappeared. Mrs. Dashner followed, and Dominick waited for Miss Dashner. When she didn't appear, he took another look at the woman in the pale blue dress. "Miss Dashner," he said, his voice sounding more strained than he'd intended.

She gave a quick curtsey, hardly even polite. "I'm ready, Your Grace." She indicated a battered valise she held in one hand. Dominick knew he should probably take his leave or offer to carry her valise or…something, but he couldn't seem to tear his gaze from her. She no longer looked like a boy. She was petite and slim, but in the faded blue muslin dress she wore, there was no mistaking her femininity. Her breasts were small but round where they pushed against the fabric of her bodice, and though her waistline was high, when she moved, he could see where it might dip in at her small waist. She had a long, pale neck that looked all the paler with her ebony hair piled on her head. The plain style left her face bare and accented her high cheekbones, her full lips, and those large green eyes fringed with black lashes.

Cat's eyes, he thought, and just as mysterious and beautiful.

"You didn't expect the dress," she said, breaking the silence.

"No."

She glanced at her mother and raised a brow, an expression he had seen many times from his siblings. It said, *I told you so.*

"It's for propriety," Mrs. Dashner said. "Rosalyn insisted on bringing her…other clothes for the work."

Dominick thought of the manuscript again and straightened. That's why he was here. He needed *The Duke's Book*, and the thief would help him acquire it. He didn't care about sick boys or struggling families. He couldn't throw a rock in London without hitting one of those. "Good. Shall we depart, then, Miss Dashner?"

She nodded and started forward, but her mother dragged her back and hugged her fiercely. "Be careful, my love. Come back to us safe and sound."

"I will, Mama," Miss Dashner managed, despite her mother's tight grip.

Watching the scene, Dominick had the urge to do more. Twenty-five pounds was not enough to help this family, not really. Instead, he opened the door and escorted Miss Dashner out.

Chapter Four

"Why did you ask that man to investigate Doctor Banting?" Rosalyn asked the next morning as soon as they were in the large traveling carriage. She'd spent the night at the duke's town house, whereupon arriving, she'd been whisked off to guest chambers, brought tea and an assortment of sandwiches, and offered a bath. She'd also been assigned a maid, who had not only fussed over her but had cleaned and ironed her dress. It was her only dress, and she wore it again this morning.

She should have slept well, all things considered, but she had worried about her mother and brothers and fretted as well about the job to be done. What did the duke want her to steal? How long would they travel? And then, as she'd been coming down the stairs, she'd heard the duke tell his secretary to look into Doctor Banting and to send him a report. What was that about?

"It doesn't concern you," the duke said, settling back on the squabs. Besides overhearing the duke ask his man to investigate Doctor Banting, she'd also heard him confirm that a groom had ridden ahead to ensure that fresh horses would be waiting at each posting house so they wouldn't be delayed and could therefore travel as quickly as possible. The duke was obviously in a hurry to reach their destination.

"As Doctor Banting is my brother's doctor, I think it does concern me," she said.

He gave her a long, hard look. He'd shaved this morning, his jaw clean of the stubble that had grazed it the night before. He'd removed his hat when he'd entered the coach, and in the daylight she could see his hair was light brown with streaks of chestnut and gold. But his eyes were what held her attention. They were still the prettiest shade of blue she had ever seen.

"I'm a curious man," the duke said at last. "I wanted to know more about Banting."

"He's one of the best in London," she said.

"So he says. I merely wondered what others might say."

She closed her mouth. It was true. She had no idea of the doctor's reputation, other than the praise he'd heaped on himself. But Michael did seem to improve under Banting's care. Didn't he?

The maid—her name was Alice—gasped as the horses started forward, and Rosalyn glanced at her. The poor girl was white as a sheet and wide-eyed. She was young, perhaps even younger than Rosalyn, with white-blond hair and pale blue eyes. She looked like she had come from Druid stock, if the old tales of Druids were to be believed. Even more important, she looked as though she had never been in such a grand conveyance before, or seated across from a duke.

Come to think of it, Rosalyn had never been in this situation either.

"Are you well, Alice?" she asked.

"Oh yes, miss." She stared out the window, then turned quickly back to Rosalyn. "Do you need anything, miss?"

Rosalyn shook her head. Just to be finished with whatever it was the duke wanted from her and to go home. "Now that we are under way," she said, leveling a look at the duke, "can you tell me where we are going?"

"Cornwall," he said.

"Cornwall? But that will take days to reach!"

"That's why I wanted to leave first thing this morning."

"And what is it you want in Cornwall?"

At this question, Alice looked away from the window. Apparently, the maid knew no more than she.

The duke looked at Alice then back at Rosalyn. "We'll discuss it later."

"When?" she pressed.

"Later."

But later, once they were outside of London, the duke vacated the carriage and rode his horse. Without the duke across from them making her nervous, Alice fell asleep, and Rosalyn stared out the window at the countryside racing by. It had been so long since she'd been out of London, she'd almost forgotten what green fields and white sheep looked like. And the air was cool and fresh, even under the heat of the summer sun.

They stopped routinely to change horses, and if time permitted, Rosalyn didn't even wait for the footman to open the carriage door before climbing down. She simply stepped away from the carriage, found a small patch of grass, and lifted her face to the sun. She could remember doing this as a child back at her home in Surrey.

"You'll freckle if you keep that up," said a male voice from behind her.

Rosalyn resisted the urge to lower her face and turn to face the duke. "I don't mind."

He was silent so long she finally did look at him. "I've never heard a woman say she doesn't mind freckles."

She shrugged. "That's because the women you know have nothing else to worry about. Freckles are not at the top of my list. Besides, I might look half alive again if I get some color on my cheeks."

"You look alive as it is."

She studied his face, but his expression gave nothing away. "Was that a compliment, Your Grace?"

"Just an observation."

"Good. Because if it was a compliment, it wasn't a very good one." She thought his lips might have quirked just slightly at that remark. "What is in Cornwall, Your Grace?"

His face clouded. He did not like this line of questioning, and the more he avoided telling her about the job he'd hired her to do, the more concerned she became. "You have to tell me at some point," she said.

He looked dubious.

"Don't you?"

"It's a book. A manuscript, to be precise," he said, surprising her. She'd thought she would have to do much more wheedling and cajoling, skills she had in abundance, as she'd finely honed them on her brothers.

"You want me to steal a book?"

"Possibly."

"Possibly? What book is it?"

"An old and valuable book."

"I didn't think it was the latest copy of Byron."

He frowned. "You have a flippant nature."

"Some people call it amusing. I like to smile, laugh, tease. I don't see the point in frowning all the time. It gives one lines." She touched his cheek to the side of his mouth. "Right here." And then she walked away, smiling because the shocked look on his face was the most amusing thing she'd seen in a very long time.

***

She'd touched him. She'd worn her gloves, so it hadn't been skin-to-skin contact, but nevertheless, she'd touched him. The sensation had jolted him, made him wonder how long it had been since someone else had touched him—someone besides his valet in the course of dressing.

Oh, he kissed his mother on the cheek when he saw her, a formal, perfunctory kiss as befitted a duchess. Nothing like the stifling hug Mrs. Dashner had given her daughter. And of course, he shook hands with men in the Lords. And there were women. He was a duke. He did not have to look very hard for a willing woman, but he had not looked in some time. And no one had touched him in any way that wasn't obligatory or dutiful in longer than he cared to remember.

That was until Miss Dashner. She'd touched him and she'd smiled up into his eyes, and his heart had jolted. He didn't quite know what to think, and so he mounted his horse and kept his distance the rest of the day. But it was impossible to keep his distance that evening. They stopped at an inn for the night, and he must dine with her, else she would have to eat in her room alone. He reserved a private room and sent word to her maid when Miss Dashner was to join him. He was in the room at the appointed hour, sitting at a table. But then he rose because his foot kept tapping. But he couldn't manage to stand still either, so he ended up pacing the room, pocket watch in hand. She was late, which annoyed him. But what annoyed him even more was that he could not seem to stop pacing. Dukes did not pace. Dukes made others pace and wait and worry.

Finally, the door opened and Miss Dashner stepped inside. She gave him a bright smile, and the annoyance he'd felt at her tardiness fled.

"Good evening, Your Grace." She looked just as fresh and pretty as she had this morning. "Have you chosen a table?" She gestured to the three empty ones in the private parlor.

"You go ahead."

"This one, I think. It's close to the hearth, but not so close as to overheat us." She passed him, and he caught the clean scent of her. She smelled of mint mingled with something floral, a clean country scent that was miles away from London. She sat and adjusted her skirts.

"Will your maid be joining us?" No one else had entered after her.

"I told her to eat with the other servants. I didn't think we needed a chaperone here. It's not *that* private. Besides, I want to continue our discussion about this book I'm to steal."

"Keep your voice down." He leaned close. "You never know who might be listening." As if to prove his point, the door opened again and the innkeeper entered. He was a pleasant enough man, tall and broad-shouldered and wearing a clean apron.

"Your Grace." He gave a slight bow. "Miss." Another. "Welcome to The White Hart. Shall I have your supper brought in?"

Dominick glanced at Miss Dashner, and she nodded.

"Very good. I'll return promptly with the tea you ordered."

He departed, and Miss Dashner raised a brow. "Tea? No ale?"

"Tea," he confirmed. He needed all his wits about him to deal with her. A moment later, the innkeeper returned with the tea and informed them it would be a few minutes until their meal was prepared.

Dominick sipped his tea, watching with amusement as Miss Dashner added three small blocks of sugar. "Shall I request more sugar?" he asked.

"Why?" She sipped her sugar laced with tea and smiled. "Did you want sugar?"

"No, but you obviously have a taste for it."

She shrugged. "I can't remember the last time I had sugar in my tea. I've missed it." She sipped again, then leaned forward. "Tell me about this book I'm to steal." Her voice was low enough that he couldn't chastise her, but he still glanced around to be certain they were alone.

"I prefer to say that you may need to assist me in acquiring the manuscript."

"I'm certain you do. Which book is it, and why do you need me to assist you?"

"Have you ever heard of the Bibliomania Club?"

"No, but I know enough Latin to understand it's a group who love books. And judging by what I know of most London societies, it's full of men so wealthy they don't have anything better to do with their money than spend it on rare volumes. Is that the gist of it?"

Dominick frowned. "We allow women."

"How progressive." Her tone was laden with sarcasm. "As I assume you only admit wealthy women, I don't suppose you want me to acquire this manuscript so I can become a member. Do you need it to retain your membership?"

"No."

"Then it's part of a competition."

"Not exactly." If he were being honest, Dominick would admit he did not want to be the only one of the three searching for the volumes of *The Duke's Book* to fail.

"Then it must be—"

"Miss Dashner."

She scowled, obviously annoyed that he'd interrupted her.

"If you will stop talking for a moment, I will explain."

"Of course!" She sat back.

Dominick opened his mouth.

"Please do explain, Your Grace," she said.

He tried again.

"I am all ears."

"Miss Dashner, if you were indeed all ears, I would have already said what I needed to say."

"Do forgive me."

It was the most insincere apology he'd ever heard. If he'd known she'd vex him this much, he would have offered her only forty pounds. "While at Oxford, I studied under an extraordinary man. He was my sponsor for the Bibliomania Club and taught me much of what I know about rare and valuable books."

"What was his name?"

He blew out a breath at this interruption. "I don't see why that matters."

"I'm only trying to make the tale a little more interesting."

"Are you implying that I am boring you?"

She opened her mouth, paused, then pointed to the door. "Oh, look! The food is here. How lovely!"

The innkeeper and a woman Dominick assumed was his wife bustled in with a tureen of soup, bread, and a variety of fresh fruits and fragrant vegetables. As soon as they departed, Miss Dashner filled her plate and bowl. Dominick supposed he should take advantage of her full mouth to speak while he could.

"The professor's name is Peebles, and he has spent his life searching for what is commonly known as *The Duke's Book*. More properly, it is referred to as *The Duke's Book of Knowledge*."

She ate bread and nodded encouragement.

"The book was commissioned by Lorenzo de' Medici sometime in the fifteenth century." He told her the history of the manuscript and about the professor's years of fruitless searching and his own discovery about his volume's possible location the night they'd met. "And so the three of us vowed to acquire the volumes as a gift to celebrate the professor's retirement. That's in about eleven days, so I need to move quickly to secure my volume."

"What is your volume about?" She put down her fork and pushed her plate away. It still held a remarkable amount of food, but her eyes must have been bigger than her stomach. "You said one was a volume on natural history and another matters of the heart. What is the one you seek?"

He was surprised she had actually been listening. "Medical knowledge. I suppose it's all rather arcane by our modern standards, but it's not the content that's important."

"I disagree. I think what's really important is your reputation. I can't think why else you would hire me to steal a book away from an old, mad earl who has nothing and no one else in his life, just to present it to a man who isn't satisfied with all he already has."

With that, she rose and walked away.

***

Rosalyn thought Stephen would have laughed at her if he'd been here. She was usually the one who argued for taking more and her brother the one who was hesitant to steal from anyone who might be hurt by the theft. But once again, she saw Stephen's point. The duke did not need this volume. He had all he'd ever need and more. The Earl of Verney, however, was a mad recluse who lived in the wilds of Cornwall—at least, that's how Tremayne had described it. What honor could there be in taking something from such a man only to give it to a man, who, though he might appreciate it, had more than enough in his life?

She was disgusted by the situation and disgusted with herself for accepting payment. Even worse, she knew she would go through with the job because Michael mattered more to her than an insane old man.

She marched for the door of the parlor, intent on returning to her room. She'd wanted to know what the job entailed, and now that she did, she'd rather not hear any more or have to look at the man who'd hired her to do it. But just as she lifted the latch, the duke's hand slammed the door closed again.

"What are you about, sir?" She rounded on him.

"I haven't given you leave."

Of all the pompous, asinine... "I didn't ask for leave. I took it. Now, kindly remove your hand from the door and allow me to return to my room."

His hand didn't budge. "You wanted to know the details of the job you'd been hired to do. Now you know."

True. And now she was forced to think how to bring the duke's plan to fruition. How to convince him of its inefficiency without raising his ire—raising it further?

"Well, I wish I didn't know these details. There's no honor in what you're asking me to do."

"You're a thief. You don't possess any honor anyway."

She inhaled sharply. A cold rage settled like a lead ball in her belly, and she stepped away from the door. "I have more honor in my little toe," she said, her voice quiet and steady, "than you have in your entire body."

"Don't be ridiculous."

"You think money or a title makes you honorable? No, it's who you are inside"—she tapped his chest—"that makes you honorable. It's what you do when you lose your money, when you lose your title, that shows your true mettle."

"So I suppose that means your true mettle took the shape of a thief." He grasped her hand and pushed it away from his chest. "Everyone knows there's no honor among thieves."

"And that shows just how *little* you do know. Now, out of my way." This time when she lifted the latch, he didn't stop her.

The next morning, she didn't speak a word to him or even glance his way. She simply climbed into the carriage and slammed the door behind her. Alice jumped. "Is anything wrong, miss?"

"Why would anything be wrong?" she said with false cheer. "It's a beautiful day to do evil."

And, in fact, the day had dawned bright and clear. The sun shone from a cloudless cerulean sky, and a mild breeze kept the afternoon from becoming too warm. Tremayne did not stop at a posting house for a midday meal. He had ordered food from The White Hart to be sent along, and they ate as they traveled. By three in the afternoon, the night she had spent tossing and turning and the novelty of a full belly meant her eyes crept closed. Alice lay sprawled and snoring on the seat across from her, and Rosalyn didn't see any reason not to emulate the maidservant's example. She sank down and was almost asleep when she heard the loud whinny of a horse and the words no traveler wants to hear.

"Stand and deliver!"

Rosalyn caught her breath but resisted the urge to spring up and peer through the open curtains. She heard the rumble of hoof beats, and then the carriage slowed, and she knew there could be only one explanation. The highwaymen had surrounded them, forcing the carriage to halt.

"What is this about? Move aside and allow us to pass, or I will make you sincerely regret it." The duke spoke loudly and confidently, but in her opinion, not altogether intelligently. Now that the carriage had stopped, she slid to the floor and pressed herself against the door. If anyone peered inside from the side where the bandit's voice had come from, they would see only Alice, who was still sleeping. If one of the highwaymen looked in from the other side, he'd see her, of course. From the angle where she crouched, Rosalyn couldn't see any men outside that window, but the shadow of a man—whether the duke or a highwayman, she didn't know—spread out over the floor of the carriage.

"Give us your valuables, and no one will be hurt," the same man who'd spoken initially ordered.

Please just give him what he wants. Don't be a fool.

"You are the one who should worry about injury. I will say it one last time. Turn around and go back the way you came." Obviously, the duke was a fool.

Rosalyn flinched when she heard the sound of a cocking pistol.

"Hand over your valuables, or I put a pistol ball in your head."

Rosalyn couldn't allow this to go on. The duke would be dead if she didn't intervene. Not that she cared about him, but how would she claim her remaining twenty-five pounds?

Stealthy as a cat, Rosalyn crept across the floor of the carriage and pressed the door latch down. The door clicked open, and she parted it just enough to peer out. There were two highwaymen on this side of the carriage, but one pointed a rifle at the coachman, and the other was in the rear, his attention on the duke and the bandits' leader. She could see why the highwaymen had chosen this spot for an ambush. Trees grew thickly along the road, creating a dense canopy overhead and making this stretch darker than most they'd traveled thus far. But the landscape also worked to her advantage.

Pushing the door open a little more, Rosalyn squeezed out, hands first, and slipped underneath the carriage. Reaching up, she closed the door with a soft click.

"What do you have in that carriage?" the highwayman was asking now. She'd evacuated just in time. From under the conveyance, she spotted his horse's hooves moving closer to the window where she'd hidden. He was peering inside and seeing only Alice. "Who are you?"

"J-just a maidservant," Alice answered. Her voice was thick from waking from sleep.

"Are you traveling alone in there?"

The pause lasted impossibly long. Rosalyn closed her eyes and held her breath until Alice said, "Yes."

"Good girl," Rosalyn muttered, then slid across the dirt road. She had only one dress, and it would be ruined after this. The things she did for this idiot duke. Reaching the edge of the carriage frame, Rosalyn reached for the nearest horse's leg and pinched it hard. Just as she'd expected, the horse startled and reared.

"What the devil?" the highwayman called. But the distraction proved enough for the duke. She saw his horse move close to the leader's, and then the duke knocked the man off his animal, jumping down after him, punching him hard, and then hauling him up to use as a shield. Rosalyn snaked forward until she was just beneath the coachman's box, then wedged herself slowly into the space to the side and waited.

"Lower your weapons," the duke called, "or I shoot him."

Rosalyn's brows rose with appreciation. He'd obviously managed to snatch the highwayman's pistol. He wasn't as much of an idiot as she'd thought.

"Go ahead!" the man with the rifle pointed at the coachman called back. "I'll shoot you right after."

The rifle swung toward the duke, and Rosalyn jumped up, landed with a crouch on the box, then leaped forward and knocked the rifle out of the bandit's hands. She fell forward, rolled, rose to her feet, pivoted, and scooped the rifle into her hands. Pointing it at the two bandits still seated on their horses, she strode forward.

"Hello, gentlemen. How lovely of you to provide me targets for my daily practice."

Chapter Five

Dominick was half afraid he'd hit his head. He could not be seeing what he was seeing. Miss Dashner had just appeared from nowhere and disarmed the highwayman who'd held a rifle to his coachman's head. And now she strode along the road, rifle cradled in her arm and at the ready, as though she knew exactly what she was about.

Perhaps she did.

All was silent for two heartbeats, and then one of the highwaymen swung his pistol in her direction. Dominick felt his heart stutter as though a pistol ball had been driven into it.

"Put that down, chit, before I blow it out of your hands." He cocked the hammer.

Dominick swore when she paused and then did as he asked, lowering the muzzle of the weapon.

"Now bring it here," the highwayman called, while the others chuckled.

"You want it?" she asked. "Get it yourself." She tossed the rifle aside, and then, so quickly he could barely follow her movements, she scampered up a tree and disappeared into the foliage.

"Where did she go?" the bandit called, while the man she'd disarmed dismounted and went for the rifle. A shot rang out, and everyone froze.

"Hands in the air!" John Coachman called out, raising the rifle he always kept tucked under his box. Immediately, the man who'd leaped off his horse closed his eyes, clearly regretting his rash behavior. He'd not only lost his rifle but he was without a quick means of escape. Assuming the rifleman also had a pistol, the odds were now even—two armed highwaymen against Dominick and the coachman. Dominick still held the leader, so he would make a poor target. But if anyone fired at the coachman, it would take time for Dominick to shove the leader away, aim, and fire. He didn't have the advantage.

The leader must have been thinking along the same lines. "There's no need for anyone to die today. Give us your money, and we'll be on our way."

"How about we keep our money and none of you have to die?" Dominick answered. One lesson he had learned from his father was to never admit defeat.

Dominick heard a hammer cock and glanced wildly about to try to determine if another highwayman had been in hiding and might be about to fire, but all he saw was a blue blur drop down from the trees. The highwayman nearest him tumbled off his horse, and John Coachman shot the one in the road, who was reaching in his coat, in the arm, causing him to fall to his knees. Dominick didn't stop to think. He shoved the leader aside and ran to Miss Dashner. The highwayman she'd landed on had shoved her off, and she'd rolled away into an immobile heap. Panting, the bandit she'd taken down rose to his feet and stumbled toward his fallen pistol, but Dominick grabbed his shoulder, spun him around, and punched him hard in the jaw.

"Let's get out of here!" the leader called and ran for his horse. The other followed suit. Only the man the coachman had shot still lay in the road.

Dominick knelt beside Miss Dashner, who hadn't moved. He placed a hand on her arm. "Miss Dashner? Miss Dashner?"

Slowly, she turned her face toward him and opened her eyes. "Am I shot?" she whispered.

"I don't think so. I think you hit your head when you tumbled off the horse with him." She had a small red bump on her forehead.

"That explains why my scalp feels as though a dagger is lodged inside. Too bright out here." She closed her eyes again.

The outriders ran to Dominick's side. "One of you check on that bandit." Dominick indicated the man who now lay in the road. The coachman hadn't moved from his box, focused as he was on keeping the team calm and still. "And you, open the carriage door. I want to put Miss Dashner inside." Dominick reached to lift her.

"I can carry her, Your Grace."

"No." He lifted her, noting she didn't weigh much more than a child. She batted his hands away at first, then laid her head on his chest. He placed her in the carriage, and the maidservant, who'd been cowering on the floor, lifted her head.

"Your Grace! Are they gone?"

"Yes. You're safe, but your mistress has been injured."

"I'll see to her."

"Good." Dominick wanted to move again as quickly as possible. There was no knowing when or if the highwaymen might return. The man the coachman had shot was bleeding from the arm. The outrider had tied a tourniquet about the injury. "Bind his hands and put him in the coach. We'll take him to the mayor in the next town."

The horses were checked, the bandit placed in the coach, and Dominick sat beside him. He wouldn't leave the ladies alone with a highwayman. An hour later, they'd deposited the would-be thief with the mayor and Dominick had reserved rooms at an inn called The King's Rest. It was much earlier to rest than Dominick had wanted, but they'd all had enough for the day.

After supper, which he'd eaten alone, as Miss Dashner hadn't been well enough to come down, Dominick went to her room and tapped on the door. His brows rose when Miss Dashner opened the door herself. When she saw him, she opened the door wider and moved aside, an indication he was free to enter. "Come to chide me for climbing trees?"

Dominick peered into her small chamber. "Where is your maid?"

"I sent her to have supper with the other servants. I couldn't stand her fussing anymore. Are you coming in, or shall we converse in the doorway?"

It would have been more proper to converse in the doorway, but she was in her night rail—at least, he thought that was what she wore under the large wrapper she tugged about herself. He didn't want everyone to see her in her wrapper. Not that he should see her either, but now that he'd already seen her, a few more minutes seemed inconsequential. Not to mention, from what he could see, the night rail was a thick, voluminous white sack. Not much to see.

"I'll come in." He stepped inside, and she closed the door then indicated two chairs. A teapot sat on the small table between them.

"Would you like tea? I have sugar left." She gave him a mischievous smile and sat.

He couldn't help but smile back. "No, thank you." He sat across from her. The red bump on her forehead had faded to a dull pink. "How is your head?"

"It feels like it did when one of my brothers whacked me when we were children, but I'll survive. The tea helped."

"Then would you care to explain to me what the devil you thought you were doing?"

She rolled her eyes. "I wondered when the lecture would come. You can't even wait until I'm well again."

"You're well enough."

She scowled. "No sympathy. You're as bad as my brothers."

"You might have had plenty of sympathy. You almost died." He realized he was practically yelling and lowered his voice. What was the matter with him? He never raised his voice.

"That is a gross exaggeration. I bumped my head. Nothing more."

His jaw dropped. "Miss Dashner, you snatched a loaded rifle from a man intent on using it, faced highwaymen with firearms, then jumped from a tree onto the back of another armed man. You should have stayed in the carriage."

"Then we'd all be much poorer."

Oh, he resented that implication. "I could have handled the highwaymen. My men and I have done it before."

"I had the element of surprise on my side. Besides, you didn't hire me to cower on the floor of the carriage."

He rose. "I didn't hire you to get yourself killed!"

"Because then you might never acquire the book."

"No! Yes. I mean, you frightened the hell out of me today."

She studied him as though she were a painter and he the subject. "Are you saying you care about me?"

"Of course I care about you."

She set her tea cup down and raised her brows playfully. "Really? Your Grace, this is all so sudden."

He realized what he'd said and had to qualify the statement. "I mean, I care about you as an employer cares for his employees. I don't want any of my people injured."

"I see. So if Alice had done what I did today, you would be lecturing her."

"Alice would never do what you did today."

She rose and stood before him. "I think that's why you like me. I surprise you."

He took a step back. "I don't like you." But he remembered how his heart had seized when he'd feared she'd been shot, and it hadn't all been because he'd hired her to get him the manuscript. There had been genuine fear and a need to protect her.

"Not even a little?" She took a step closer to him.

"This conversation is inappropriate." He moved back again.

"It is. If I told you that you impressed me today when you grabbed the leader of the highwaymen, would that also be inappropriate?"

"I—" He'd impressed her?

"It wouldn't be suitable for me to mention how handsome you looked, how dangerous."

"Miss Dashner." But he didn't know what to say. Heat radiated from his neck to his cheeks, and he feared he was actually blushing.

"Have I embarrassed you, Your Grace? Surely you know you are handsome."

He fumbled for the door latch behind him. When had he turned into a bumbling schoolboy? "I should go so you can rest. We'll leave at first light tomorrow."

"I'll be ready."

He opened the door, then hesitated. "I owe you an apology." He looked back. Her brows were high and her expression one of surprise. "Yesterday I insinuated you had no honor. I was wrong." Dominick stepped out. "Good night." Closing the door, he walked quickly to his own chamber. There, he closed the door, leaned against it, and took a deep, deep breath.

***

The man she'd teased and made blush the night before, the man who had apologized to her for insinuating—ridiculous, he was not so subtle—she had no honor had disappeared in the morning. He'd been replaced by a stern, demanding oaf who rattled off a litany of orders. As most of them didn't have to do with her, Rosalyn climbed into the carriage, shut the curtains, and closed her eyes. She hadn't slept well the night before. She blamed it on the dull ache in her head and the lumpy bed, but her overactive mind had been part of the problem as well. Why had the duke blushed? She'd been teasing when she asked if he liked her.

What if he did like her?

Did she like him?

Of course, she didn't like him. But several hours later, when she couldn't quite stop herself from opening the curtains to peer out at him, she had to admit she was at least attracted to him. And she hadn't lied when she'd said he'd impressed her. He was more competent than she'd thought, and whether or not she'd placed too much emphasis on his lecture the night before, he did care enough to check on her.

That afternoon, the duke ordered they have a picnic lunch, as he didn't want to take the time to stop at an inn and dine. He'd had The King's Rest pack food for them to eat, and one of the footmen laid it on a blanket in a sunny field a little ways off the road.

"Join me, Miss Dashner," the duke said. It wasn't a question.

She sat, straightening her now stained blue dress. Alice had tried to clean it, but she'd been unsuccessful. They dined on cheese, apples, bread, and a very good wine, and there were more bundles to unwrap. Rosalyn wasn't particularly hungry, though.

"How did you come to love books?" she asked.

The duke paused and looked up from the glass he was refilling with wine. "I always enjoyed reading. It filled the long hours in the country."

She held out her glass for more wine. "I never read in the country, only when we came to Town. It seemed there was never enough time to climb all the trees or chase all the butterflies I wanted when I was in the countryside."

"I was never one for climbing or chasing. The heir to a dukedom is expected to behave with decorum, even at a young age."

That sounded awfully tedious. "But surely you had friends you might ride with or plan battles. My brothers would spend hours lining up their toy soldiers when we were young."

"My brothers are quite a few years younger than I. My sisters are closer in age, but they were only interested in dolls."

"And what of your friends?"

He sipped his wine. "I didn't have many friends growing up. The other children seemed to think I was…"

"Dictatorial?" she offered.

"No." He frowned.

"Overbearing?"

"No."

"Arro—"

"Miss Dashner." His voice held a sharp edge. "I was about to say they considered me too staid. I actually preferred reading."

He looked so offended, she put her hand on his arm. "I was only teasing. My brother Michael is a great reader as well. I think there is no better pastime, as literature not only entertains but educates."

Slowly, he pulled his arm away. "I do think you are the only person who has ever teased me, Miss Dashner."

"That is a tragedy, Your Grace. You should be teased more. Anything that makes you smile is to be encouraged. You have a very attractive smile."

His expression was one of absolute shock, and before she could laugh or he could say something to annoy her, she rose and strode back to the carriage. She had never met a man she could so easily surprise or whose reaction she enjoyed as much.

Several hours later, when they'd stopped at another inn and finished dining in the private parlor, the duke informed Rosalyn they would reach Cornwall and The Temples on the morrow. He had stubbornly resisted her attempts to make him smile all evening, even blushing at one point, but she couldn't resist trying again.

"And when we arrive, do we charge the keep immediately, or do we attempt negotiation first?"

"This is not a game, Miss Dashner. I will call on the earl, and if I cannot persuade his staff to allow me to speak to him, then I will request your assistance."

"And that's when I'm to scale the wall of the fortress, breach its defenses, confront the earl, and persuade him to meet you in the drawing room."

"More or less."

"Why don't I just find the library and steal the volume? It seems more efficient."

They were seated across from each other at a small table near the hearth, and he leaned forward. "I don't want to steal the volume."

She leaned forward, so close they were almost nose-to-nose. "Then why did you hire a thief?"

"I like to be prepared for all eventualities." He hadn't moved back to put distance between them as she'd expected. And now she was the one who felt heat rising to her cheeks. "In any case, our time together is quickly coming to an end."

She nodded. "Then I suppose if you want to kiss me, you should do it soon." Rosalyn couldn't have articulated why she'd said it. She hadn't planned to say such a thing. She hadn't even known she wanted him to kiss her, but as soon as the words were out, she both regretted them and hoped he would act on them. What would it be like to watch this carefully controlled man succumb to passion? And wouldn't she like to be the one with whom he succumbed?

Ridiculous thought. Now she'd only made things awkward between them. She started to move back, but he lifted a hand and ran a finger along her cheek. The light, simple gesture made her freeze. Perhaps things were not quite so awkward as she'd feared.

"I have been wanting to kiss you since…"

"Since you first met me?"

"No."

"Since you first saw me in a dress?"

"No." Before she could speak again, he placed his finger over her lips. "Since I watched you stroll down the middle of a road, facing armed highwaymen."

"Oh, that," she mumbled, his finger still on her lips.

"I've never met a woman like you. I think I can hardly be blamed for wondering what it might be like to kiss such a woman."

She wrapped a hand around his wrist and drew his finger down. "I think you should try it and see."

"Here?"

"Yes."

"Like this?"

"Yes. No choreography required."

"But—"

She kissed him. All she had to do was lean forward and press her lips to his. Yes, the table between them was inconvenient. Yes, someone might enter at any moment and interrupt, but Rosalyn did not intend to lose her opportunity.

His mouth was warm and soft, and the act of placing her lips on his was quite nice. Initially, he seemed frozen in shock, but then he kissed her back, and that was quite nice as well. She didn't have much experience kissing. She'd kissed a few boys here and there, but never a man. Never a duke. Now she'd have something to tell her grandchildren one day.

She drew back, smiling, but her grin faded when she saw the intensity of the duke's look. "Did I do something wrong?" She rose. He rose as well and rounded the table. Now she was the one who took a step back. "Shouldn't I have done that?"

"It was a bad idea."

"Why?"

He stepped closer, and she stepped back again.

"Because now I want more."

"More?"

"More."

She stepped back again, but this time, he caught her arm and hauled her forward, against his chest. "Any farther back and you'll step into the fire," he explained.

She glanced over her shoulder and saw she'd almost backed into the hearth. "Thank you."

"It was no trouble." He was solid and warm against her, his strong arms enveloping her. "And since you are here." He bent, and though she could see he intended to kiss her, she couldn't quite believe it until his lips took hers. This kiss was not at all like the one they'd shared a moment ago. Then, she'd been teasing, testing him, really. But he was not teasing. His mouth took hers with a fierceness that surprised her and made her body catch fire all over. She half feared she had stepped into the hearth after all, because quite suddenly she felt so very, very warm.

His hand skated up her back and cupped the curve of her head, where her hair was pinned, then he deepened the kiss. She knew what he wanted, though she'd never done this herself. But she'd seen others do it. She opened her mouth to allow him entrance, and when his tongue licked inside, she gasped.

He pulled back, his blue eyes large and dark. "Should I stop?"

"Why would you stop?"

"I don't want to scare you."

"I assure you, Duke, the only thing I fear is that you won't kiss me again." The staid duke had hidden stores of passion.

With a smile that made her insides melt, he kissed her again. This time, she ventured into his mouth, her tongue tangling with his. It was his turn to catch his breath. He pulled back and looked down at her. "My name is Dominick."

"Lovely." She kissed him again, not caring what his name was, only wanting to feel his warm lips on hers again. His mouth slanted over hers, and she was not disappointed.

Until he pulled back again.

"May I call you by your Christian name?"

She rose on tiptoes to kiss him again, but he held her back, waiting for her answer.

"Yes, call me Rosalyn. And if you still feel like calling me Miss Dashner, I must be doing something wrong."

His laugh turned to a groan when she took his head in her hands and kissed him deeply. Somehow, they had moved backward, and she felt the wall press against her back. She was relieved to have something to support her. Her legs felt wobbly, and her feet had lost all sensation. There was only the two of them and the way their mouths met, lips teasing and tasting.

And then the dratted man pulled away again. He braced a hand against the wall and, panting, looked down at her. "Rosalyn is a pretty name."

Did he want to have a conversation? "Dominick is pretty too," she said, then reached up again. But he took her shoulders in his hands and held her back. "This is not the time for a conversation, Dominick."

He smiled, making her want to kiss him again. "I'd argue it's exactly the time for a conversation. Otherwise, we may do something we'd both regret."

She wasn't so naïve she didn't know what he meant, but she hadn't considered the possibility that what had begun as an innocent kiss might turn into something much, much more. And if she enjoyed kissing him this much, then how much more might she enjoy what came after? But she was no wanton, and she neither wanted to be ruined by a duke nor bear his bastard. So she lowered her arms and took a fortifying breath. "You're right. I should go to bed."

"As should I. We have a long day tomorrow."

"In that case, sleep well…" She wasn't certain what to call him now that they were no longer touching. Your Grace? Duke? Dominick? "Sleep well."

"You too, Rosalyn," he said, as though he knew her dilemma.

She nodded and made her way on unsteady legs to the door. But she didn't go immediately to her room. First, she stepped outside and pressed her hands to her cheeks and gulped the fresh air. But it would take more than a hay-scented breeze to take away the memory of his hands on her. And it would take sheer willpower to keep from kissing him the next time she saw him.

Chapter Six

Dominick stared at the ancient structure looming above them. They'd traveled through Cornwall all morning, until they'd finally reached what Dominick assumed must be the most remote area in all of England. The road—if one wanted to call it that—was flanked by cliffs on either side, and below the cliffs, the ocean slammed hard against craggy rocks worn and weathered by the centuries. Rising above it all at the end of a narrow peninsula was a gray structure with towers looming from all four corners and keyhole arrow slits cut into the stone.

"There it is. The Temples, Your Grace," John Coachman announced, sitting back when he'd halted the carriage and an outrider had opened the doors.

"Why have we stopped here?" Dominick asked. The carriage stood a quarter mile or more from the entrance to the old building.

"It's too narrow up ahead, and I don't trust the ground. Could be dangerous for the horses, Your Grace."

Dominick stepped down and surveyed the road himself. The coachman was correct. It would be dangerous for the horses and the carriage to continue. He turned to see Rosalyn descending the carriage steps. She wore a long cape that hid the male clothing she wore underneath, but he knew she was prepared to climb the wall of The Temples at his mere command.

"We walk from here," he said, turning away from her. He waved off the outriders who would have accompanied them, as well as the maidservant. The fewer people who approached the mad earl the better. In fact, Dominick would have left Rosalyn at the carriage too, but she would need a close view of the building if she had to climb it later.

Of course, now, as he walked ahead of her along the rocky path, he was rethinking that plan. He shouldn't have kissed her. He'd known it was a bad idea the moment he'd considered it, but he hadn't been able to convince himself when she stood before him. But in the cold light of morning, when he'd been apart from her for hours and able to evaluate the situation, he knew becoming personally involved with her had been a mistake. She was a servant, little more. He couldn't afford to worry about her safety. If every time he looked up at the high steep walls of The Temples, he imagined her plummeting to her death on the wet rocks below, he would never allow her to scale them. And then he might never acquire the manuscript.

The manuscript was everything, not simply because he wanted to be able to present it to Professor Peebles, though that was important. The man had searched for the volume his whole life. There was no one more deserving. But the search was about more than that. It was about proving himself as a member of the Bibliomania Club. The club stood for truth and knowledge, and Dominick wanted to contribute to those lofty purposes by acquiring a volume that would shed light on the truth and knowledge as it had been viewed in the time of the book's conception.

And, of course, he did not want to be the only one who failed. A Duke of Tremayne never failed.

Dominick glanced at The Temples again. He had to crane his neck to look up at the towers. The climb would be dangerous, and any mistake could mean a long, long fall. If Rosalyn made one false move while climbing that wall, he would never kiss her again. He would never hold her in his arms or inhale the fragrance that was hers alone.

He tried to remind himself there were plenty of other women who smelled just as sweet and felt just as good in his arms. But it wasn't any use. He'd kissed other women, touched other women, and he'd never felt the way he felt when he held Rosalyn and pressed his lips to hers.

"What shall we do now?" she asked, coming to stand beside him. Dominick realized he'd been standing before the massive oak door of the castle for several moments.

"We knock." He eyed the knocker, a tarnished gold ring fashioned into a design of a snake eating its own tail.

"Do you suppose anyone is at home?" she murmured. "It looks completely uninhabited."

"There is but one way to find out." He lifted the knocker and lowered it on the metal plate three times. The hollow sound that echoed back at them made Rosalyn shiver. Dominick resisted the urge to pull her close and reassure her. She was a servant. He was paying her to do a task. He had to remember that.

Five minutes or more passed, neither of them speaking as they stood before the door. Dominick reached for the knocker again, but Rosalyn put a hand on his arm. "Listen," she whispered.

He listened, shook his head, and then froze. He'd heard what she must have as well. A distinct shuffling sound came closer and closer. Rosalyn's hand tightened on his arm, and Dominick did exactly what his mind told him not to—he put his own hand over hers to comfort her.

Or, if he was being brutally honest, perhaps the action comforted him.

The clang and creak of locks turning and latches lifting echoed into the sunlit day behind them. But as the door scraped open, clouds seemed to sweep across the sun, casting everything and everyone into a gray gloom.

In the doorway stood a man of medium height with dark hair and dark eyes. He was dressed in black, his clothing tailored and clean. He looked every inch the typical butler. In fact, he looked so typical that Dominick did not hear him when he spoke.

Rosalyn poked him, and Dominick started. "I beg your pardon."

The butler smiled as though he were used to this response. "I said, good afternoon and welcome to The Temples. I am Payne. How may I be of assistance?"

"I've come to pay a call on the Earl of Verney." Dominick held out the card he had ready. "You may tell him the Duke of Tremayne and his companion are here."

Mr. Payne did not seem as impressed by a duke coming all this way to call as Dominick might have hoped. The butler looked at the card then back at Dominick and Rosalyn. Finally, he stepped back, opening the door wider as he did. "Won't you come inside and out of the rain?"

Dominick frowned. It was not raining. But as soon as he thought it, a raindrop plopped on the back of his neck and the boom of thunder rent the quiet. Rosalyn was staring back the way they'd come, and he turned to follow her gaze. Rain poured in sheets, soaking the horses and the outriders. Lightning flashed in the angry skies over the churning water.

"Storms arise quickly over the water," Payne said. "Does your traveling party require shelter? I'm afraid we have no stable. It washed away several years ago."

That meant Dominick would either have to let his party stand in the rain or send them back two miles to the last vestiges of civilization. He faced Payne. "They'll be fine."

Rosalyn gave him a disapproving look but didn't speak. She stepped into the grand foyer just ahead of him, her neck craning to look up at the vaulted ceiling. The foyer was easily two stories, a massive chandelier hanging from the highest point. It was not lit, but the sconces burning around the chamber meant that the chandelier shed a wide shadow over the center of the floor. Though dark and musty, as many old buildings were, The Temples looked clean and well-kept. If a madman did indeed reside here, his madness had not interfered with basic housekeeping.

"This way," Payne said, lifting a candelabra. He led them out of the foyer and through a dark, windowless passage. The passage ended before an arched wooden door. Payne extracted what looked like a skeleton key from his waistcoat, fitted it in the lock, turned it, and opened the door. The interior was dim, and when Rosalyn began to enter, Dominick grasped her shoulder, holding her back. He wasn't certain whether this was a prison cell or a parlor, and though it might be customary to allow a lady to enter ahead of him, he felt the need to protect her.

Dominick strode into the room, noting the hearth had been lit, warding off some of the chill. It was not a prison cell, but a small parlor, furnished with tapestries and ornate wooden chairs that would have looked at home at the table of King Henry VIII. Rosalyn entered next, followed by Payne with the candelabra, which he set on a side table. "Would you care for refreshment?"

"No," Dominick said. "We'd like to speak to the earl as soon as possible."

"Of course." Payne smiled. "If you will excuse me for a moment, I will see if the earl is at home."

He left the room, closing the door behind him.

"Why do I have the urge to check whether he locked us in?" Rosalyn whispered.

"This isn't a prison, Miss Dashner," Dominick said, reminding himself as much as her.

"It looks quite normal on the inside," she said, moving about the room to examine the tapestry. "I thought there would be spider webs and rusty suits of armor."

Dominick wouldn't admit it, but he'd envisioned far worse. "You are allowing your imagination to get the better of you."

"I don't have an imagination," she countered. "And I didn't imagine that storm that was summoned when you knocked on the door."

"There is nothing supernatural here, Miss Dashner. My family owns at least one castle almost as old as this one, and though it is dark and crumbling, there are no ghosts."

"Oh, that's comforting. Now you have me worried about ghosts," she grumbled. He almost smiled, then caught himself. He must treat her as a servant. Not as a woman he found clever and amusing.

"What is your opinion of the outer walls?" he asked, bringing his attention, and hopefully hers as well, back to the problem at hand.

She looked away from the tapestry and met his eyes with her lovely green ones. "I can climb them," she said, sounding confident. "They're not smooth or sheer. There are plenty of bricks that might serve as hand- and footholds. The problem is that there are no outer windows, only embrasures, and even I am not small enough to squeeze through one of those."

"Then there was no reason for you to come." He felt a sense of relief. She couldn't enter The Temples by climbing the outside. She would not have to risk her life doing so.

"I didn't say I couldn't do it," she snapped. "I only said there are no entrances on the walls. The roof is another matter."

"What do you mean?"

"This was a fortress meant to repel attacks coming from land or sea, correct?"

He nodded, beginning to see where she was leading him.

"There must be turrets along the roof where archers could stand and rain arrows down upon invaders. That means there is a way in from the roof. I only need to climb that high."

Dominick did not want her to climb that high. He did not want to watch her small body dangle above him, while he stood on firm ground below and watched in safety. He couldn't allow it. "Rosalyn," he began.

Someone tapped on the door, and Dominick spun around, expecting to see the old earl, but he was greeted by an ancient woman carrying a silver tray. The tray looked heavy and the woman small and frail, and Rosalyn immediately raced to the servant's aid. "Let me assist you!"

"I have it," the old woman said in a papery voice. "I can still carry a tray or my name isn't Clothilde Wright."

Rosalyn glanced at Dominick, and he strode forward, taking a table with him. "Set it here, Mrs. Wright," he said, placing the table directly in front of her.

"Thank you, sir." She smiled, lifting the mass of wrinkles on her face. "Are you certain this is convenient? You should have tea by the hearth—" She made to lift the tray again, and Dominick shook his head.

"This is perfect. Please do not trouble yourself."

She wiped her hands on her apron. "Very well. Is there anything else you require?"

They hadn't asked for the tea and sandwiches on the tray. "Just the earl, Mrs. Wright. Can we expect him soon?"

"The earl?" The old woman looked confused. "I don't know. I was told to fetch tea for our guests. So nice to have guests. And what a handsome couple you make. Is this your honeymoon?"

Dominick felt his cheeks heat. "No," he said at the same time Rosalyn all but shouted, "No!" He scowled at her. "We came to call upon the earl."

"We have so few guests. The last couple was touring Cornwall on their honeymoon. Such a nice young man and a pretty lady. They didn't stay long."

"Did they meet with the earl?" Rosalyn asked.

"Oh, no. They wanted to tour the castle, but we don't show The Temples."

"Why not?" Dominick asked.

"Oh, too many ghosts, I suppose."

Rosalyn's eyes grew wide, and she moved closer to him.

"Just ring for me if you need me." Mrs. Wright indicated the bell-pull. And then she was gone.

"Do you think she was serious about the ghosts?" Rosalyn whispered when they were alone.

"No. I'm sure she's trying to scare us away. Stories like that will deter other travelers from stopping by and expecting a tour."

"But we don't want a tour. We want to speak to the earl."

"And I am afraid that is not possible," a voice said from the doorway. Payne was back. "The earl is unwell today and will not see visitors."

Dominick had been expecting this. "Did you tell him the Duke of Tremayne is calling? I've come a long way."

"I did, Your Grace. The earl sends his regrets."

"I'll return this evening."

The butler nodded. "That is your choice, Your Grace."

Dominick extended his arm to Rosalyn, and the two exited. Outside, the rain still poured. "May I offer you an umbrella, Your Grace?" Payne asked. Dominick glared at him.

"Don't bother."

When the door to The Temples closed behind them, Rosalyn huddled under the scant protection provided by the overhang. "The lightning and thunder have stopped," she said. "If you make a show of walking out to the carriage, I can slip around to the back."

"Why would you do that?"

"You hired me to scale the walls if you couldn't speak to the earl."

Dominick had to resist the urge to pull her close and protect her. "The rain is coming down in sheets. It's too dangerous."

"I've climbed in the rain before. I can do it."

"You'll wait," he ordered and, taking her hand, pulled her to the carriage with him.

***

Rosalyn did indeed wait. She waited three days. The duke went back to The Temples time and again, but was turned away regardless. They had taken lodgings in the only inn within ten miles, and as there were only two rooms, she and the duke shared a wall. She could hear him railing to his servants that time was running out and he was no closer to acquiring the book than he had been.

Soon, they'd return to London empty-handed. Then what would happen? Michael's declining health required that she earn the rest of her fee, and she wouldn't receive it if she didn't make certain the duke acquired the volume he sought. The duke hadn't said as much. In fact, he'd said very little to her the past few days. She was relatively certain he was avoiding her. They hadn't taken a meal together since the night they'd kissed. Did the duke worry being alone with her would be awkward, or did he simply not want to see her again? Perhaps she was the only one who thought again and again about the kiss they'd shared and wished for another.

Truth be told, she wished for more than that. The duke was a good man. He could be rigid at times, but he could also soften and make her smile. He was good to his servants, the horses, and the innkeepers. He was a kind man. A good man. Letters arrived from London, and he took hours each day to pen responses addressing every concern his stewards might have on any of his vast properties. Yes, he might be mad for this book, which to her seemed rather unimportant, but as hobbies went, collecting books was far less detrimental than gambling or whoring.

When she heard him return from The Temples on the third night, heard the disappointment in his voice as he addressed a servant, she knew what she had to do. The duke might very well feel obliged to pay her, even if she didn't acquire the book for him. She didn't want his charity, didn't want to take advantage of his goodness.

Rosalyn pulled the shutters open and looked out. A half-moon sat in a partly cloudy sky. She might have wished for more light, but it was not raining and it was the best she could hope for. Rosalyn dressed in her male clothing, slipped down to the stables, saddled one of the horses, and made her way to The Temples.

She tied the horse far enough back that he would not be spotted, then approached the narrow, treacherous path alone. The Temples was dark. No lights burned in the windows, and she relied on the light from the moon when it wasn't buried behind clouds. Finally, she'd made her way to the rear of the building. A path wound around the castle, but it was less than a yard wide and ended in a sheer, rocky drop down to the tumultuous seas below. Peering over the edge and into that churning black water, Rosalyn knew if she fell, no one would ever know what had become of her. Her lifeless body would be washed away and never seen again.

So she would not fall.

She extracted her gloves from her pocket and pulled them over her shaking hands. These were one of the tools she'd packed in her valise. Then she changed into her special shoes, leaving her worn half boots at the base of The Temples. She walked along the edge of the building, feeling for handholds, and when she found a likely spot to begin, she took a deep breath.

"For Michael. Always Michael," she whispered to herself, calming her racing heart. "And this time for Dominick too."

When she was calm and steady, she reached up and began to climb. It was difficult work, and she was perspiring within minutes, but it was also familiar. Her body knew what to do. Her hands sought alcoves or outcrops even without her having to think about it, and her toes curled and wrapped around ledges too small for anyone but the most astute to note. She climbed without looking up or down, without wondering at the passage of time, without any thought but of the next place for her hand or foot. When it began to rain, she did not think of the weather. She took more care, now that the stone was slick, but she did not hesitate.

Several times, she lost her footing and dangled above the crashing waves below. Rosalyn wouldn't allow fear to enter her mind. She held tightly with her hands and slid her foot along the wall until she found a better foothold. Then, when she'd regained her balance and caught her breath, she inched upward.

She had no idea how long she'd been climbing when she felt the turret at the top of the building. It might have been minutes or hours. The important thing was that she'd made it. She grabbed the edge of the stone wall circling the top of the building and hauled herself up, her arms shaking with the effort. But the section she'd grabbed began to crumble under her hands, and she realized she'd made a novice mistake. She'd been so relieved to see the end in sight, she hadn't tested the strength of the next handhold. She slipped down, and stone scattered past her, falling for so long she did not hear it land. She had one chance to grasp the next closest section of wall. If it too was weak, she'd go sliding into the sea like the loose rocks.

Her hand slipped as more of the wall dissolved, and she grasped for the section above her. She caught it with the tips of her fingers and closed her eyes, praying it would hold. When it didn't disintegrate, she pulled up. This was the hardest part. Her arms were tired, and now she had to haul her entire body up and over this wall. With a grunt of effort, she lifted herself high enough to release the footholds. Sweat poured down her face, and her arm muscles felt as though they might ignite from the fiery pain lancing through her. Though there was little to give her traction, she tried to use her feet to give her more leverage. Gradually, she worked one elbow over the wall, then the other. She rested for a moment, then swung her legs over and fell onto her back.

The rain felt good on her face, cooling her skin. She didn't know how long she lay there, but when she rose and checked the location of the moon, she realized she had probably been climbing no more than an hour.

Standing, Rosalyn tucked her gloves back into her coat and pushed her wet hair off her face, securing the loose pieces into the queue at her nape. She spotted a doorway and started for it.

Time to meet the mad old earl.

Chapter Seven

Dominick blamed himself for not knowing she'd left earlier. It was his own fault for not prioritizing his correspondence, as was his usual practice. But the servant who'd delivered the letters had placed one from the bailiff of his property in Yorkshire on top, and Dominick had not looked at any others in his haste to read that one.

As matters in Yorkshire were still tenuous, he had replied at once and only glanced through the rest of the letters when he'd finished with the most pressing issues. That was when he'd spotted the letter from his secretary in London and one from Mrs. Dashner. It was addressed to him, not Miss Dashner, which he supposed made sense, as it was easier to find a duke than a young lady of no real name or fortune.

He opened the one from his secretary first and read it quickly, nodding the entire time. It seemed Dominick had been right to question the credentials of Doctor Banting. The secretary wrote that the man had few if any credentials and had a reputation for being a fraud and a cheat. In the opinion of the men the secretary had interviewed, consulting with Banting would do a patient more harm than good. Dominick would show it to Rosalyn—Miss Dashner, he had to stop thinking of her so informally—immediately. When they returned to London, she could dismiss the fraud and engage the services of a doctor who could provide real care for her brother.

Dominick supposed the letter from Mrs. Dashner was to ask for more money. These were the sorts of letters he was used to receiving. He only hoped the woman didn't attempt to threaten him with some lie, like he'd stolen her daughter away. He would not show this letter to Miss Dashner. She had not once asked him for so much as a ha'penny. She didn't appear to have any designs on him. After that kiss, he'd worried he'd opened himself up for a seduction ploy. Would she try to repeat it when they'd both be discovered, then force him into proposing marriage? But she'd made no attempt to be alone with him or to steal into his room at night, even though it would have been incredibly simple, as their doors were but a foot apart.

He certainly hadn't slept well thinking about her on the other side of the wall they shared. He could hear her conversing with Alice, her maid, and he tortured himself, wondering if she was dressing or undressing. She might be petite, but he had held her close enough that he knew she still had a woman's figure. He would have liked to explore those curves and dips at leisure.

Pushing his lustful thoughts away—again—he opened Mrs. Dashner's letter and then stood. He couldn't have been more wrong about the reason the woman had written. It wasn't any sort of scheme. It was a notice that Michael Dashner had taken a turn for the worse. Mrs. Dashner did not expect Rosalyn to rush home, as she knew her daughter had given her word to the duke, but would he ask Miss Dashner if she wanted to pen a final note to her brother in case he passed away in her absence?

"What rot!" Dominick said and swore. He'd do far better than asking Rosalyn to pen a note. She needed to see her brother in the flesh. He'd take her home immediately. Tonight. And he'd pen a note now to have the best doctor he knew, his own, sent to tend to Michael.

He was almost to the door when he realized that leaving now meant he would not acquire *The Duke's Book* in time for Professor Peebles's retirement. The volume on arcane medical knowledge would not be among those presented to the man. Dominick would be the only one who failed in the quest to reunite the complete set.

And he didn't care a whit.

The revelation stunned him. He'd rarely cared for anything more than he cared for his collection of books, but he had come to care for Rosalyn. He'd come to anticipate her smile, look forward to her morning greeting, long for her kiss. Dominick couldn't imagine seeing the light go out of her eyes if her brother died. And it wouldn't happen if he could prevent it.

He could find *The Duke's Book* another time. But at the moment, it was as useless as the medical knowledge it contained.

A moment later, he tapped on Rosalyn's door. When her maid opened it, he realized he hadn't thought what he would say. But he wasn't given time. The maid looked as though she had been crying. "Your Grace, thank the Lord you are here. I cannot find her."

"Miss Dashner? You mean, she isn't in her room?"

The maid shook her head. "No, Your Grace. I left for a few minutes to bring the tea tray down to the kitchen, and when I came back, she was gone."

"How long has she been gone?"

"An hour at least, Your Grace."

Dominick clutched the door's casement. "Why didn't you tell me sooner?"

The maid shrank back at his harsh tone. "I-I'm sorry, Your Grace."

Dominick wasted no more time. He all but ran down the stairs and into the common room. A few questions told him no one had seen Miss Dashner in the inn. In the stable, no one had seen her either, but a quick check showed that one of the horses was missing, as was some tack.

She'd left. She'd taken the horse and left.

And since she didn't know about her brother, there was only one place she would go. The image of her battered and broken body lying on the rocky ground beneath The Temples flashed in his mind.

"No!" he yelled and began to shout orders.

***

Rosalyn descended the narrow, stone steps leading into the castle keep, then spent some time at the base working to wedge the door open. If she'd had to guess, she would have estimated it had been at least a century since the steps had last been used and the door was stuck closed. Fortunately, it wasn't locked. And when, with bruised shoulders, she finally opened it, she stepped into a small, dark corridor. The door was at the end of a short, bare hallway with a wooden floor. Closing the door behind her, she made her way along the hallway and encountered another set of stairs. These were wider and cleaner, and she descended them, electing to explore the first landing she reached rather than continue into the bowels of the keep.

The landing led to a small antechamber, which was ornamented with rugs, dark wooden furnishings, and tapestries. No fire burned in the hearth, and with her wet clothing, she shivered in the chill. But she could feel a warmth emanating from the door at the other end of the chamber. A light shone through the sliver of an opening, and she could hear the crackle of logs in a hearth. She tiptoed to that door and peered inside.

A figure sat near the fire, small and clad in black. The woman—Rosalyn surmised it must be a woman—was bent over with concentration. It was a posture she knew well from watching her own mother sewing by firelight. As though sensing she was being observed, the woman turned. "You should have stayed away," she said.

***

Dominick found the horse Rosalyn had ridden some little ways from The Temples and tethered his own beside it. The rain made the rocks on the path slick, but he ran at full speed, his eyes scanning the stone walls of the structure for any sign of Rosalyn. When he didn't see her on his approach, he ran around to the back, slowing to take more care on the narrower path. But he did not see her. Holding his breath, he looked over the cliffs to the ocean below. In the darkness and rain, it was impossible to discern anything about the shapes below. They might be bodies or boulders. If she'd attempted to climb the building and had fallen, she was certainly dead.

His heart clenched as he considered that possibility. He didn't care about the damn *Duke's Book* any longer. He wanted only to see Rosalyn smile at him again. He wanted only to know she was alive and well.

Dominick ran to The Temples's entryway and hammered the knocker on the door. After five minutes, his arm ached, but he wouldn't give up. If he had to break the door down, he would gain entry. He had to believe she had made it inside. Finally, Mrs. Wright opened the door. She looked white-faced and wide-eyed. "Your Grace, may I help you?"

"I'm looking for the woman who accompanied me on my first visit. Have you seen her?"

The housekeeper's eyes lowered. "You will have to return later, Your Grace. There's been a disturbance." She began to close the door, but Dominick wedged his shoulder against it.

"I'll not come back later. If she is here, I demand to see her."

"No one is to be admitted," she said, as though repeating a refrain. Dominick had heard enough. He took the older woman by the shoulders and gently moved her aside before shouldering his way in.

"Where is she?" he asked. "Tell me."

Mrs. Wright looked up.

Dominick took the steps two at a time.

***

"I suppose it was too much to hope that I would get away with it," the woman said, setting her sewing aside and rising. She was perhaps sixty, slim, with gray hair and a straight spine. She was only a few inches taller than Rosalyn, but her rigid posture made her seem taller. "I do wish you would have listened to Payne and gone away."

"I'm sorry," Rosalyn whispered. "I don't mean to bother you, but I need to see the earl."

The woman sighed. "You cannot. He's dead."

Rosalyn took a step back. The woman's words rang in her ears like a warning. *I suppose it was too much to hope that I would get away with it.* Had she *killed* the earl?

"Now you know my secret," the woman whispered.

Rosalyn shook her head. "I don't know anything. I can leave now. No one has to know I was here."

"I wish that were true," the woman said sadly, "but you will tell someone. I don't know how I kept it a secret this long."

"I won't tell your secret." Rosalyn began to back into the cold, dark antechamber. "No one need ever know I was here, Mrs.—"

The woman raised her steel-gray brows. "I am Lady Verney, and you have no need to be afraid. I didn't kill him."

Rosalyn let out a long sigh. Thank God. This was the earl's wife, and she hadn't murdered her husband. But then, why did she keep his death a secret?

"Payne!" the countess called. A moment later, the butler stepped out of the shadows behind Rosalyn, making her jump. "Please bring us tea. This young lady must be cold and wet. Miss—?"

"Dashner," Rosalyn said.

"Miss Dashner, do come sit by the fire with me."

With Payne blocking her only escape, Rosalyn did not see how she had much choice. She entered and sat in a chair not far from the one the countess had occupied when sewing. The countess sat as well, and Rosalyn fidgeted, unsure what she was to do next. "I am sorry for your loss," she said to break the silence.

The countess raised her brows. "I'm not! The man was mad, had been mad for twenty years. His death was a blessing, I will tell you that. He used to run about here babbling nonsense. Half the time, he was dressed in rags or wore nothing at all. We couldn't keep any staff and spent a fortune on doctors. Nothing helped."

Rosalyn could understand that feeling.

"The last doctor wanted to take him away, put him in some sort of institution." The countess shook her head. "I wouldn't allow that. He died at home, in his own bed, among people he knew."

"That is a blessing," Rosalyn murmured.

"Yes." The lady's eyes sharpened. They were a pale blue, rimmed with gray. "But you didn't come to hear about my late husband's last days. You are here on behalf of the heir, that awful, awful boy."

Rosalyn blinked in surprise. "No. Actually, I don't know anything about any heir. I'm here for a book."

"A book?"

"Yes, a manuscript, actually. It means a great deal to a friend of mine. He's willing to pay for it. He's a collector of sorts, you see."

"I see." She rose. "Come with me, Miss Dashner."

Rosalyn's belly clenched. "It doesn't matter anymore. If you just let me go—"

"You'll want to see the library," the countess said. "Come with me."

Rosalyn saw no option other than to follow the countess out of the room and down a stairway. The lady descended, then paused, indicating Rosalyn should precede her when they reached the next floor. Rosalyn's heart thudded in her chest. She was so close now. Could the countess really possess *The Duke's Book*? In a matter of seconds she could acquire it and give it to the duke. Then he would pay her the remainder of the fee. Her family would be safe for a little while. And the duke would have what he wanted. She knew how much this manuscript meant to him.

Rosalyn veered in the direction the countess indicated and paused before a closed door. The lady extracted a long key from a chain at her waist and unlocked the door. Then she lifted the burning sconce at the door and shone it into the room. Rosalyn gasped just before she heard the shout.

***

"Rosalyn!" Dominick called. "Are you here? Rosalyn!" Dominick ran up the stairs, his voice echoing off the stark walls. Suddenly, he heard what sounded like a woman's voice. He paused, listening.

"I'm here. In the library."

The library? Dominick took several more steps, pausing at a landing where light flickered from the open door of a chamber. He moved toward it, pushed the door open, and there stood Rosalyn and another woman, an older, handsome woman.

Behind them was a large library filled with dozens of gleaming shelves, all empty. Not a single book or piece of furniture inhabited the room. It was completely empty, shining from recent polish and echoing hollowly at the sound of his footsteps.

Dominick ignored the room and strode to Rosalyn.

"May I present—"

He took her into his arms, pulling her tightly against him. She was wet and shivering, but she was whole and she was alive. He held her close, his eyes closed as he rested his chin on the top of her head. "You're alive," he murmured. "I thought I'd lost you."

"I'm alive," she murmured. "But the earl isn't so fortunate."

He pulled away from her, looking down at her face. She looked so pale and cold. "Tell me you didn't climb the walls to gain entrance. Tell me you knocked on the door like a sane person."

Her dark brows drew together. "You really have no faith in my abilities, do you? Of course I climbed the walls."

He wanted to laugh and to shake her all at the same time. "Of course you did. Never again, do you hear me? I don't want to lose you."

"But I did it for you. I know how much the book means to you—"

"Nothing," he said. "Nothing compared to your life."

"Should I leave you two alone?" asked the woman.

Dominick stepped back, and Rosalyn made the introductions. "Lady Verney, this is the Duke of Tremayne. Duke, the Countess of Verney."

"I am terribly sorry to inconvenience you like this," Dominick said. His gaze drifted back over the library. The very empty library.

"I suppose there is nothing for it now," the countess said. "I am found out, but you will at least allow me to explain before you contact the proper authorities."

"There's really no need," Dominick said, thinking of the letter from Mrs. Dashner.

"Please," the countess said. How could Dominick refuse?

They were led to a drawing room and served tea and biscuits. With the rumble of thunder in the distance and the flash of lightning at the windows, the widow began her tale.

"I married very young," she said. "Younger even than you." She nodded to Rosalyn. "The earl was quite sane then, and we were fortunate to have many happy years. But there was sadness as well. We had no children, and we always knew The Temples would go to a virtual stranger, especially as time passed and nephews and brothers passed away, some of them meeting sad ends. When the earl's real descent into madness began, I had the lawyers discover the identity of the next heir. It took almost two years to unravel the lineage and follow each branch to its conclusion. Finally, they located a cousin, a third or fourth cousin to my husband. I summoned him here, and one meeting told me all I needed to know."

"What was that?" Dominick asked, drawn into the story despite his impatience to be gone.

"The man was worthless. He'd spent his life and his fortune on women and gambling. He had the gall to ask me for money when he came, and when he looked at The Temples, all he saw was what he could sell to finance his liaisons. I told him no and sent him back to London. I would have prayed for the earl to live forever if it would mean that awful man never inherited."

"But he didn't live forever," Rosalyn said.

"No." The countess was steely-eyed again. "He died a year ago."

Dominick could not quite stop the quick intake of breath.

The countess closed her eyes in shame. "It is shocking, I know. We told no one, Mrs. Wright, Payne, and I. We buried him ourselves and told visitors he was not well."

"But you must have known you could not keep his death a secret forever," Rosalyn said. Dominick was glad she'd spoken, her voice soft and full of understanding. He was rather less understanding. As a duke from a long, prestigious line, he considered the countess's actions a shocking betrayal of her rank and station.

"I knew, but I needed time. Time to put The Temples's finances in order, time to make sure that it would stand, no matter what that awful man tried to do to it. And I confess, I took that time to sell some pieces I should not have, pieces that by all rights should go to the next earl. But I couldn't allow paintings I loved or the books the earl had collected to fall into that man's hands. I couldn't!"

Now Dominick did understand. He too felt a kinship with his books. He would not want them sold off or ignored should anything happen to him. "What did you do with them?"

"I sold them to a W. Stanley & Co. I researched dealers, and he has a very good reputation. I know he will see they are well taken care of."

Dominick knew the man, and he could not fault her choice.

"But my actions were not wholly unselfish," the countess said. "Because of the sad state of our finances, I was left with very little when the earl died. I have a niece I can live with, but she is not wealthy. I would hate to be a burden to her, and I will admit I took some of the money and put it away for myself."

Dominick felt Rosalyn's gaze on him, and he knew she saw her own mother in this woman. Here was another widow who would be thrown out, through no fault of her own, and all but left to her own devices. Well, Dominick had no desire to bring any further misfortune on the countess. "My lady," he said, "I cannot say I agree with your actions, but neither do I have any desire to reveal them. I believe I speak for Miss Dashner and myself when I say that your secret is safe with us."

She stared at them for a long moment. "Bless you. You will not have to keep it long. That I promise you."

Dominick held up a hand. "I want no details, my lady. As far as I am concerned, we never gained entrance to The Temples." He rose. "And to that end, I think we had better take our leave."

The countess rang the bell. "I'll have Payne see you out."

Dominick bowed and took Rosalyn's arm. As he left the drawing room, he felt his dream of acquiring *The Duke's Book* slip away. He could find W. Stanley. He could instigate a search for the manuscript there, but the thought gave him no pleasure.

He no longer had any appetite for *The Duke's Book*. It was as though *The Duke's Book* had been a child's sweet, and Dominick's palate had matured. He couldn't understand why it had ever meant so much to him.

"His lordship loved the library," Payne said as he escorted them through the foyer. "He spent hours inside."

"I can see it would have been impressive," Dominick said. "I think the earl would be pleased that his books are now in good hands." He could feel Rosalyn staring at him in shock, but he'd explain later. Now he wanted her safe and at his side.

Chapter Eight

When they'd returned to the inn and she'd changed into dry clothing and been warmed with brandied tea and a blazing fire, the duke knocked on her door. Alice answered, and Tremayne indicated the maid should stay. Rosalyn began to rise, but he waved her down. "I know you want to talk about what you saw at The Temples and what we should do about it, but we don't have time for that right now."

A cold shard of worry pierced the warm calm she'd settled into. "What do you mean?"

He held out two letters, and she recognized her mother's handwriting on the first immediately. She ripped it from his hand and began to read, even as he explained. "We leave for London tonight, as soon as you're able. We'll travel straight through, only stopping to change horses. If we're fortunate and make good time, we can be there in two days."

"Michael," she murmured. Then, "Yes. I need to go. Now." She tried to rise, but the duke put a restraining hand on her shoulder.

"Alice, pack Miss Dashner's things and your own. We are leaving as soon as you are ready."

Rosalyn nodded, relieved Alice was there. Her thoughts were in turmoil. She could think of nothing but Michael.

"There's something else," the duke said. "The doctor Michael has been seeing is a fraud." He handed her the other letter. "If you'll allow me, I'll send my man to you. He's excellent."

She shook her head. "I doubt we could afford—"

The duke held up a hand. "You needn't worry about payment. I'll take care of it."

It was a refrain she heard often in the next hours. Once underway, she thought to ask what they should do about the dead earl. The duke told her he would take care of it. Indeed, he took care of everything, for which she was grateful. She could do little but fret about her brother. She'd never felt so helpless. The last leg of the journey was particularly trying, as she knew they were close, but she feared she wouldn't arrive in time. And then she was home, falling into her mother's arms.

"Michael?" she asked as her mother hugged her tightly.

"He's fighting, darling," her mother whispered. "We haven't given up hope yet."

The duke's doctor was there, and Rosalyn was disturbed to see that he'd thrown away all of Michael's tonics and potions and eschewed bloodletting. He ordered the boy fed nourishing broth and given fresh air and sunshine.

"You want us to take him from his bed?" Mrs. Dashner asked.

The doctor, an older man, with a thick head of white hair, nodded vigorously. "These small rooms fill with coal smoke, which is why his condition worsened when he came to Town. The boy needs fresh air and food.

The countryside would be perfect. In the meantime, the steam from a bowl of hot water and mint leaves will help open his lungs."

Rosalyn and her mother exchanged looks. They would not be able to take Michael to the countryside, but Rosalyn had long believed that the meager diet Doctor Banting had prescribed made Michael weaker, not stronger.

In the next few days, Rosalyn had little time to think of anything but nursing her brother. Stephen and Daniel carried him outside and walked him around, while Rosalyn and her mother heated water and made broth. After a few days, the duke's doctor returned and pronounced the boy looking better already.

Rosalyn agreed. Michael was sitting up and able to stay awake longer. His breathing was still labored at times, but his cheeks had regained some color.

A knock sounded on the door, and when Stephen opened it, the duke was there. He bowed and greeted everyone, his eyes never leaving Rosalyn. She felt herself blush and had to look at the floor so no one would notice.

"Ah, Your Grace," the doctor said. "I was just telling the family that Master Michael seems somewhat improved, but the real improvement will only come if they take him out of the city for a time. He needs fresh air."

"And we do appreciate all you have done for us, Doctor Cavender," Mrs. Dashner said, "but I'm afraid we don't have the means to leave London at present."

"I'll take care of it," the duke said.

Rosalyn's head snapped up at the same time her mother said, "Pardon me?"

"I'll take care of it. My Hampshire estate is the closest. I can send a coach and attendants first thing in the morning."

"But we couldn't possibly impose on you to do such a thing!" Mrs. Dashner argued.

"It is no imposition at all," the duke said. "In fact, I insist." He bowed again, and after the doctor took his leave, the two men departed. Rosalyn waited all of fifteen seconds, then raced after them.

"I'll be back in a moment, Mama!"

The doctor had climbed into his gig, and the duke was striding toward his own conveyance when Rosalyn reached the street. "Your Grace! Wait!"

He turned toward her, then motioned to the footman to close the door. He approached so they stood under the awning of the printing shop below her flat. "How can I possibly thank you for your kindness, Your Grace?" she asked. "It's too much."

"It's not nearly enough," he said. "I should have offered sooner. I should have sent Cavender to your family sooner. Rosalyn." He cleared his throat. "Miss Dashner, I know speaking now, with your brother so ill, might be impertinent, but once he is well again, might I have the pleasure of calling on you?"

She frowned. "You're calling on me now, Your Grace." He was acting so strangely.

He shifted. "Then might I have the privilege of courting you?"

Rosalyn's jaw dropped. "Courting?" she said, before her throat closed in.

"You needn't answer now. And your answer has no bearing on my earlier offer. Your family is welcome at my Hampshire estate regardless, but if you do not wish it, I will not trouble you there with my presence."

It had taken her a moment—several moments, in fact—to understand him. She supposed it had been too long since she had been in such genteel company, and she'd forgotten some of her social graces. But she understood now. The duke wanted her. The duke… Was it possible he admired her as much as she did him?

"Are you saying you want to court me?" she asked.

"I want to marry you."

Her jaw dropped.

"I apologize if my frankness offends you." He stepped back.

"But you are a duke!" she spluttered.

"And you are the daughter of a gentleman."

"Yes." Rosalyn smiled. "I am." She closed the distance between them.

Seeming bolstered by her smile, he took a breath. "I thought perhaps you might need some time to know me better, to come to care for me, before we discuss marriage."

"I'd like that. But what about the manuscript? Don't you need to make inquiries?"

He waved a hand. "That's all settled. It is not worth my time if you are amenable to my presence in Hampshire."

Her breath caught at the thought of seeing him in Hampshire, walking with him, talking with him, teasing him…

"I am amenable, Your Grace. Would it be forward of me to say I am eager?"

"I like it when you are forward," he murmured.

"Then might I add that, far from finding your affection offensive, I welcome it and return it, Your Grace."

"Dominick," he said.

She smiled. "Dominick. I have only hoped you might feel the same."

He smiled back, a true smile that lit his entire face. Lord, but he was impossibly handsome when he was happy. "Then I will call on you when you and your family have settled in at Hampshire." He took her hand and kissed her knuckles.

"I'd like that, but I have one request before you take your leave."

He arched a brow.

"I want more than a kiss on my hand, Dominick. You will think me wicked, but I haven't forgotten the kiss we shared at the inn."

"Nor have I."

"Will you kiss me now?"

He looked about. "Here? On the street?"

"Exactly."

"I thought you'd never ask."

He took her into his arms and kissed her, and though it was brief, it was every bit as perfect as that first kiss. When they parted and he looked into her eyes, Rosalyn knew they would share many, many kisses in the years to come.

Acknowledgments

Thanks to Kelly Snyder for suggesting the title of this novella.

And much appreciation to Grace Burrowes for saving me from sickening readers with my original plot. (And no, I won't tell you what it was. Well... I might if you write to me and ask.)

Of course, thanks goes to Carolyn Jewel as well for being such a fabulous co-author and to Miranda Neville for her help with the book's theme and concept.

And I want to acknowledge Joyce Lamb for her stellar copyediting. She tries to make me perfect, but if there are any mistakes, they're still my own. Same goes with Sarah Rosenbarker, who proofed the manuscript. I always send her what I think is a flawless manuscript, and she always finds more mistakes. Thanks, Sarah.

Taken by the Duke

Chapter One

"Why does she not have a net?" Henry Selkirk, Viscount Bexley, asked his secretary. "If she falls, all of our hard work will be for naught. The papers will carry the story of a dead performer, not that of the celebrations for the Regent's birthday and Britain's triumph over the French."

"Yes, my lord," Morton said, scribbling notes in a small book he carried. "Make certain the rope walkers have a net," he murmured to himself.

Henry couldn't understand why the woman would venture out on a rope without a net in the first place. Did she want to die? He certainly did not want to see her pretty face battered and bruised.

But then, Henry did not understand the motives behind what most people did. Especially those who *enjoyed* taking risks and confronting danger. Henry walked on, his dark gaze scanning the walk and the parade of couples passing by. "Half of these lamps are not lit, Morton," he said. "It's far too dark. No wonder the pickpockets are so bold."

"Too dark. Yes, my lord."

Henry heard a giggle and a shush from one of the shadows. It was not difficult to ascertain why the walks were not properly lit. Lovers wanted darkness for privacy. And they could have their privacy and their damn walks back just as soon as the prince's celebrations were ended. God knew Henry wanted them over more than anyone.

He tossed a glance over his shoulder.

Except perhaps Morton.

"Keep up, Morton."

"Yes, my lord." He all but jogged to keep pace with Henry's long strides.

"I did not ask for this position, Morton," Henry said, walking on. He'd been to the pleasure gardens just outside of London half a dozen times over the past fortnight. He'd signed contracts with musicians and with George Barrett, who owned Vauxhall Gardens. The prince wanted a masked ball, a concert with fireworks, and a grand ball. His Highness had tapped Henry to organize it all.

"I wanted no part of this business, Morton."

"No, my lord."

"I went to see Prinny on an entirely different matter."

"At the urging of the Lords, sir."

"Yes. I was to speak to him about his overindulgent spending. Do you remember, Morton?"

The secretary nodded. "It was a ploy, my lord."

"It was an outright trick. Send the new man into the lion's den."

"It's not your fault you are newly a viscount, my lord."

No, that was his cousin's fault. The damn man had to fall from a horse and break his neck. And this after his fathers and brothers had succumbed to a fever. Why was no one in his family ever careful? But after a string of unlikely deaths that led Henry—far, far down in the line of succession—to inherit, Henry was beginning to believe this viscountcy was cursed.

If only he hadn't happened upon the prince and his cronies when the group had been planning celebrations for the victory of Waterloo and the prince's birthday. When Henry had suggested to the prince that he might try to economize, the prince had agreed.

"Right you are, Bexley, and you are just the man I need."

Henry had looked from the prince to Prinny's friends Lord Alvanley and Sir Lumley, known to his friends as Skiffy. The gentlemen had looked as perplexed as Henry. "Your Highness?" Henry had finally offered.

"You will help me economize, Bexley. I hereby declare you the...er—" The prince looked to his friends for inspiration.

"The royal master of ceremonies, Your Highness," Alvanley had suggested with a smug smile. Henry had never liked the baron.

The prince clapped his hands. "Exactly!"

Henry had been the prince's royal master of ceremonies for precisely sixteen days, four hours, and almost forty-five minutes. In that time, he had persuaded the prince to combine the Waterloo and birthday celebrations, convinced the prince that he did not need to arrive nightly in a bier borne by four elephants, and counseled against a champagne fountain.

And the celebrations were still wildly overbudget.

And now that Henry was finally seeing the gardens at night, as they would be during the celebrations, he was demanding lamps be lit, rope walkers be protected, and more security brought in. All of those changes would require blunt. But Henry hadn't been to Vauxhall Gardens since he'd been a child, and he hadn't realized how much it had deteriorated. The last thing he needed was for the prince to be harmed or accosted during the festivities.

Henry and Morton rounded a corner, entering a particularly gloomy area of what was known as the dark walks. Thus far they'd encountered only lovers seeking privacy, but now they came face-to-face with a group of youths harassing a young man.

Henry cursed under his breath in frustration. This was exactly the sort of thing he wanted to avoid. He was no coward and would not run from the situation, but how he wished he were home in his library, safely ensconced before a fire.

One boy of about eighteen, with hair blond enough that it shone in the darkness, pushed the smaller lad so he stumbled. The boy was caught by another of the gang, this one a few years older and a ginger with a flat face full of freckles.

"What is this about?" Bexley demanded. It seemed the sort of thing he should say.

"Help me, sir," the boy said before the ginger pushed him down to his knees.

"Shut yer potato hole." The ginger put his hands on his hips, and the other three youths closed ranks behind him. Henry wasn't overly concerned. These might be thugs, but they knew better than to lay hands on a nobleman. That was a hanging offense. Still, he was careful and alert.

"Release that lad at once."

"And if I say no?" the ginger asked.

"Then I'll call for one of my constables and have you escorted from the gardens. It's time we removed all the riffraff. You, sir, are no longer welcome here."

"Is that so?" the ginger asked. The boy on his knees, small and slim, trembled and ducked his head.

"Yes."

"You got that turned about, guv. You're the one not welcome." He looked at his friends. "What do you say we give the nob a farewell present?"

The youths nodded, and Henry braced for a fight. He'd been in his share of fights on the streets of London when he'd been young and reckless and a fool. Now he preferred to avoid risky situations (there was the cursed viscountcy to think of), but he really had no choice at the moment. He couldn't leave this defenseless boy, and it was too late to walk away. Henry was careful but not a coward.

It had been some time since he'd had a scuffle, but he was confident he could inflict some damage and cause enough of an uproar to attract one of the constables.

But to Henry's shock, the ginger didn't come for him. Instead, he yanked the lad up from his knees. Henry barely saw the glint of the blade before it slammed down and into the boy's belly. The boy bent over, blood dripping onto the ground. He took a step and fell.

Someone screamed, possibly Morton, possibly the boy who'd been gutted. Henry rushed forward to catch the boy. But the lad staggered away and crumpled into a twisted ball.

"Morton, call for the constable," Henry ordered, yanking out his handkerchief. He bent, taking the lad by the shoulders. "How bad is it? Here, let me staunch the flow of blood." As he reached for the lad, the boy rolled slightly onto his back. He looked up at Henry with a look Henry couldn't quite decipher, and then he reached up and wrapped his arms around Henry's neck.

"Now!" the injured boy yelled, sounding far too robust for a lad who was bleeding profusely from a belly wound.

"What—" Henry began.

"My lord! Watch out!" Morton called.

Cursed, Henry thought.

That was his last thought before all went black.

***

He came awake slowly and by degrees of pain. First, he was aware of the pain in his head. The back of his head throbbed incessantly, causing a roaring in his ears akin to that of a riotous mob. Next, he was aware of the pain in his shoulders and his arms. He tried to touch his aching head, but his hands were bound behind his back. Moving them at all shot pinpricks of agony up and down his skin. The limbs had obviously fallen asleep and objected to waking up.

His back was the next area of discomfort he noted. He lay on something hard and cold, and his back protested not only his hands digging into it but the unyielding floor. Finally, he tried to open his eyes.

That was the worst pain yet. The room was poorly lit, but even the gloomy lamplight made his head swim. He snapped his eyes shut again. After a few moments, the roaring in his ears seemed to subside and he was aware of voices.

"Where's Hedgehog?" a low, melodious voice asked.

"The boys have him outside, Duke. Do you want him?"

"Bring him in."

Footsteps came alarmingly close, the boards near his head quavering in response. Then a door opened, and all was silent except for the sound of footsteps, lighter and more muffled. Perhaps a man walking on carpet? Henry was half tempted to open his eyes again. He was prepared for the light now, and the ache in his head was tolerable, barely, but if he opened his eyes his captors—it was becoming increasingly clear that he'd been abducted and bound—would know he was awake. Better to feign unconsciousness and plan his escape.

Escape?

How was it he, Henry Selkirk, was planning an escape? This sort of thing was not supposed to happen to him. He was too cautious to be abducted, damn it.

Footsteps shook the floor, and a door creaked open. This time, multiple footsteps sounded as well as some sort of scuffling. "Let me go!"

Henry risked cracking his eyes open and saw a man struggling in the grips of the ginger and the blond he'd seen at Vauxhall earlier that night. Through a small window, he noted it was still dark outside, so he hoped it was still the same night. He had no idea how much time had passed or how long he'd been unconscious. He also had the quick impression of a small, dark room paneled in wood before he closed his eyes again. The man between the thugs from the gardens must be the one they called Hedgehog. With a short, round body and spiky hair, he looked like a hedgehog.

Hedgehog emitted a string of inventive profanities before a low, silky voice interrupted. "You did this to yourself, Hedgehog."

"Duke, I can explain."

Duke. This was the second time someone had called the leader—the man with the honeyed voice—*Duke.* But if he was a duke, what was he doing with criminals from Vauxhall? And why would he keep a viscount tied up?

"I don't want your explanations. You stole from me, and you know the price for that."

"No, Duke. Don't!"

Hedgehog was moving away from Henry and toward the duke. Too late, Henry realized he knew this because he'd opened his eyes and was staring straight at the man they called Duke. And he was no duke at all. He was the lad from Vauxhall, the one who had been stabbed. His white shirt still bore the crimson stain of blood. The stabbing must have been a trick, a lure to reel Henry in. But why had they wanted him and—more important—what would they do with him now?

Henry stared at the scarlet on the man's otherwise well-made linen shirt. Of course, it wasn't the lad's blood at all. Just another part of what must have been a plan to abduct him and—what? Ransom him to his family? Kill him? Keep him hostage until after the prince's celebration?

Oh, very well. The last one was wishful thinking.

The lad they called Duke raised a brow, or so it seemed. His face was shadowed by the cap he wore. "You might as well quit pretending to sleep," he said. "Go ahead and sit up. You'll want to see this. It will save me the trouble of devising a new lesson for you."

Henry struggled to roll over, not an easy feat with his hands bound and nothing to use for leverage.

"Red," the duke said. "Help him."

"I can do it," Henry all but growled. He'd just as soon look a fool than accept any help from the ginger who had smashed his head.

"Hurry up. I don't have all night." The duke reached for an iron bar and slapped it into one small hand—pale, delicate hands that looked as though they should play the violin or sip tea.

Or pick a pocket. The best pickpockets prized their hands above all else.

Henry rose to his knees, a sickening lump forming in his belly.

"No, please. No!" Hedgehog begged, tears and snot running down his face. Red, the ginger, held his right hand down on a lovely cherry wood desk. It was bare of paper or ornamentation, but for the pistol on one corner.

Seeing that Henry was on his knees and had a view of the desk, the one they called Duke nodded. Then he looked at Hedgehog. "If you ever steal from me again," he said, his low voice menacing, "I'll put a pistol ball in your brain. Count yourself lucky tonight."

Hedgehog could do nothing but blubber.

The duke raised the black bar. Henry wanted to look away, but he wouldn't give this duke the satisfaction. With a soft thud and a crunch of bone, the bar landed on the vulnerable flesh. Hedgehog screamed. Henry winced. The hand had a visible dent in it, and blood welled from the flattened fingers.

"Get him out of here," the duke said.

Red yanked the sniveling Hedgehog away, the man cradling his injured hand to his chest. The duke looked at the blond. "Clean this up." He gestured to the desk, which had a splatter of blood arcing out from where the hand had lain.

"Yes, Duke." The blond jerked his head toward Henry. "What about him?"

"He comes with me."

Henry was still staring at the spray of blood on the once lovely wood of the desk when the duke jerked him to his feet. For a small man, he was surprisingly strong. He reached into his boot, pulled out a knife with a long, sharp blade, and slit the rope binding Henry's ankles. Unlike his wrists, his ankles had not been bound tightly, and Henry had no trouble standing on his own.

Until the duke grabbed the rope around his wrists and pushed him forward. "Hey!" Henry yelled when he stumbled.

"Shut up and walk." Such a melodious voice for such harsh words. And then when Henry didn't move fast enough, the duke grabbed the bindings on his wrists and yanked upward.

Henry bit back a scream. He wouldn't cry like a child, but the duke would pay for that little act of cruelty.

If Henry made it out of here alive.

"Walk," the duke ordered.

Henry walked. Using the bindings, the duke guided Henry like one might a horse through what Henry realized must be a tavern or inn. He heard voices in a room to his left and what sounded like the clink of glasses. And he smelled the yeasty scent of freshly baked bread and the thick, rich odor of broth simmering with potatoes and spices. He hadn't eaten since breakfast, and his stomach let him know that, along with his head and his back, it had complaints.

Finally, Henry was marched up a back set of stairs such as servants might use and pushed before a wooden door. He glanced down the hallway and saw other doors were nearby, all shut like the one before him, and the hallway ended abruptly. It was closed off from the rest of the building. Which meant if this was an inn, situated in Lambeth or another of the areas near Vauxhall, the patrons using it might have no idea of the presence of these criminals.

It was an ideal lair for these delinquents. And, of course, this was an unfortunate realization, because it would make finding Henry that much more difficult. That was, if anyone was even looking. For the first time, he wondered what had happened to Morton. Had they taken his secretary, or had the man been able to get away to alert a constable, or perhaps call in the Bow Street Runners?

"Barbara," the duke said. "Open the door."

"Open it yerself," came the tart reply.

The duke stiffened, pulling back on Henry's bindings. Henry was tempted to point out that he was not the one who'd offended.

"Barbara, open it now, or you can spend the rest of your days on your back in a brothel in Seven Dials."

"What nonsense," came Barbara's reply, spoken in a carefree voice. But a moment later, the door opened, and Henry looked down and into the face of a plump and pretty blond woman. She had dark blue eyes and pink cheeks, shown to advantage with her golden hair pulled into a pile on the top of her head. Her ample hips, large bosom, and bright smile spoke of a woman who enjoyed life.

Her smile turned curious as she took him in. Her gaze flicked behind him, presumably to the duke. "I didn't know you had company." She arched a brow, then winked at him. Henry merely stared at her in bewilderment, a constant state of late.

"He's not that sort of company," the duke answered, pushing him forward.

"I see that now," Barbara answered, obviously noticing his bindings. She shut the door and moved in front of him again, her gaze more assessing. "But what can he have done? A tall, dark, and handsome gentleman like this?"

Henry wondered if Barbara was attempting to incite the duke's jealousy. Was she his lover? She'd been waiting in what must have been the duke's bedchamber. It contained a wardrobe, a dressing screen, and a large bed.

"That's not your concern. Leave us," the duke ordered.

"Leave you?" Barbara looked appalled. "Alone? With him?"

"We have matters to discuss. Private matters," the duke added.

"I'd like to discuss the state of your shirt, Duke."

At what Henry surmised was a warning look from the duke, Barbara stepped back and raised her hands. "But we can discuss that later. Set it outside, and I'll collect it for washing. As for him"—she gave Henry one last look—"you'd better keep him tied up."

"I intend to."

Barbara left them, and Henry tensed, not certain what would come next. "I don't know who you are or what you want, but I won't speak to you until I know whether my secretary is alive and well."

The duke cocked his head, his face in shadow and partly hidden by the cap. "The balding man you were with?"

Henry gave a slight incline of his head.

"He's with the men in the servants' quarters. I imagine he's more comfortable than you at the moment."

"I want to see him."

"I don't care." The honeyed voice had an edge to it now. "You aren't in charge here, Henry Selkirk."

"How do you know my name?"

"How do you *not* know mine?" The duke put his hands on his hips as if in challenge.

"I heard them call you Duke," Henry answered, but the duke waved a hand dismissively.

"My real name, Henry. You said you would never forget me."

"I said...what?" The duke was obviously delusional. "I've never met you before in my life. I'd give anything not to have met you now."

"So sure, are you?" The voice took on a different quality. It was still low and melodious, but now it had almost a teasing tenor.

And then the duke reached up and grasped his cap. With a tug, it came off, revealing short honey-brown hair tucked behind small ears, a small pale face, and large brown eyes he could not have forgotten had he wanted to.

"No." He shook his head. This was all wrong. This boy couldn't be—but it wasn't a boy. The illusion had been broken, and Henry couldn't help but see the delicate bones of her face, the slim lines of her body hidden beneath boys' clothing, and the long lashes framing the eyes.

"Kate," he said, the name sounding halfway between a prayer and a curse.

"Welcome to The Griffin and the Unicorn, Henry."

Appropriate name for the place, Henry thought, because none of this could possibly be real.

Chapter Two

"Surprised to see me?" she asked, though the look on his face answered that question easily enough. He looked more than surprised. He looked at her as though she were a ghost.

Perhaps to him she was.

"I was surprised to see you," she continued, not liking the way the heavy silence fell in the room. "I had no idea you were in line to become a viscount."

"I wasn't," he said, his voice rough, as though he hadn't spoken in years. "It should never have happened."

She circled him, wishing she could remove his bindings but not ready to trust him yet—if ever. "And yet it did happen, and now you are one of the prince's set."

He shook his head, his dark curly hair catching the light of the candles with the movement. He'd always had such thick, dark hair, the curl like spirals if he let it grow too long. Now it was cut just short enough to tousle, as was the fashion, but not long enough for her to insert her finger into a midnight spiral, as she had when they'd been children. "I barely know the prince. I was tapped to organize the celebrations——" He broke off. "It wasn't supposed to happen."

She moved before him again. "There seems to be a lot of that in your life."

"Yes," he said, his gray-blue eyes meeting hers. She'd always thought his eyes such a pretty color, especially set off as they were by his otherwise dark features. The slash of brows, the mop of hair, and now the dark smudge of stubble on his cheeks and jaw. She was tempted to touch that stubble, but she refrained. She wouldn't have liked to be touched thus if she'd been bound, and the least she could do was extend him the same courtesy.

That was about all the courtesy she had to give.

"What are you doing here, Kate?" he asked suddenly. "Why do they call you Duke? Why dress as a man? Why go to all this trouble"—he nodded at her stained shirt—"to speak with me?"

She gave a harsh laugh. "You think all of this is about you?"

His brow furrowed, and oh, but it was as adorable as it had always been. Although, he was no longer what she would call *adorable*. He was a man now—tall, muscular, and strong. If he hadn't been bound, he would have attempted to overpower her before she could blink. That kind of power and danger were far from adorable.

Which was why she should have put him in the dungeon—what they called the room in the servants' quarters where they kept rivals from other gangs and where his secretary currently resided—but she couldn't send him away without first speaking to him.

Playing with fire, her mother would have said. And yes, Kate had always been one to play with fire.

And get burned.

"None of this is about you, *Lord* Bexley."

"Just call me Henry."

"If you insist on acting like a pompous ass, I'll treat you like one, *my lord*."

"Kate—"

"You may call me Duke."

"Not likely, *Miss Dunn*. Answer me this. If none of this is about me, then why am I being kept prisoner?"

"After all this time, that is the burning question you wish to ask?"

He gave her an exasperated glance. "It seems the most pressing as my hands are numb and my arms throbbing in pain."

"I am sorry about that." And she was. "Perhaps I can find a way to make you more comfortable. But first I want out of this bloody shirt."

He closed his eyes.

She shrugged. "Bad puns. A weakness of mine." Ducking behind her screen, she shed her coat and attempted to unfasten the buttons on the shirt. Her hands shook so badly she had to pause and take a deep breath. Perhaps sending Barbara away had not been the best idea. She could have used her help now.

Kate closed her eyes and felt the sting of tears she would never allow herself to shed. She could still hear the crunch of Hedgehog's bones when the rod had come down on his hand. She was sick to her stomach at the thought of what she'd done—and yet she'd had no choice.

She knew he'd been stealing from her for months. She'd given him veiled warnings and cautions, and he hadn't taken them to heart. She was relatively certain Red also knew Hedgehog was stealing, but when one of the cubs—the youngest members of the gang—had come to her and reported Hedgehog was a thief, she'd had to act. She hadn't become the leader of the gang and a duke of the criminal underworld by allowing her own rogues to steal from her. And if she showed any sign of weakness now, any sign of softening, there were a dozen men and boys waiting to take her place.

Fear and a grudging respect kept her gang in line. She'd had to do unspeakable things to earn her position, and if she fell, all of the sacrifices she'd made would be for nothing.

Kate opened her eyes again. She hadn't enjoyed smashing Hedgehog's hand. It would mean an end to his days as a pickpocket, but she'd spared his life. He could find other work. Most of the arch rogues of the other gangs would have killed Hedgehog for less.

She'd always thought that once she had power, she could afford to be merciful. But now she wondered if her mercy toward Hedgehog—little as it was—might be the sign of weakness one of her own needed to try to overthrow her.

If that happened, she knew what she'd be forced to do.

Kate blew out a breath and started on her buttons again. A deadly calm settled over her. This was her life. She couldn't close her eyes, couldn't turn her back, couldn't trust anyone. The moment she thought she was safe, that she had "made it," was the moment she'd be the most vulnerable.

And now she'd found Henry Selkirk. Her old friend Henry had grown up and become a viscount. What must it be like to wake up one morning and realize you were a lord? A titled peer of the realm. He had everything—wealth, safety, power—and he'd done nothing to earn it.

Kate didn't think the two of them could be more different.

It hadn't always been that way.

She pulled the shirt over her head and dropped it on the floor.

"You can't keep me here, you know." Henry's voice floated across the room, reaching her behind the screen. "I'll be missed."

"That must be nice," she said, untying the string holding up her trousers. "Having people who miss you. Your wife? Children?"

"I meant my staff," he said.

Ah, so no wife and children, then. Why should that please her? It wasn't as though she wanted to marry him. That would be a girlish fantasy, and she'd long outgrown those.

"If you cooperate, you will be safely tucked into your mansion in Mayfair in no time."

"I don't live in a mansion."

Was it her imagination, or was his voice closer than it had been a moment ago? She remembered she'd cut the bindings on his ankles, which meant he was free to move about her bedchamber.

"Don't you?" She turned and caught him watching her from the other side of the screen. "My lord, a gentleman would never spy on a lady."

His face reddened slightly, and he turned so his back was to her. She stared at him, surprised at his behavior. She'd expected him to argue, to point out she was hardly a lady. Instead, he'd treated her with courtesy. Her gaze dropped to his hands, which had turned purple. She had certainly not given him the same courtesy.

She allowed her trousers to drop to the floor, then started unwinding the bindings that flattened her breasts.

"I wondered how you had managed to hide your figure," he said. She looked up at him, but his back was still turned. "I should not have been so curious."

She shrugged, forgetting he couldn't see her. "I don't have much to hide."

"Forgive me, but from the glimpse I had, that's not quite true."

Now it was her turn for her cheeks to heat. And suddenly her nakedness made her feel vulnerable. She reached for the silk wrap she wore when she was alone—one of her few luxuries, her few nods to her femininity—and pulled it on, cinching the belt tightly.

She removed the daggers from her boots, then toed them off. Taking hold of his bindings, she cut them. It was probably a mistake, but she didn't want to look at those purple hands any longer.

With a hiss, he lowered his hands to his sides, then groaned as he rotated his shoulders and crossed his arms over his chest. She winced in sympathy. She'd been bound before, and she knew the pain of numb limbs coming back to life. Giving him a private moment to recover, she strode across the room and poured a glass of wine from an open bottle. She sipped it, then shrugged and poured him one as well.

She turned. "Drink this. You can probably use it."

His handsome face was contorted, but he gave a quick nod. "Thank you," he said through clenched teeth.

"Don't try anything," she added when he began to move toward her. "I still have my knife, and I know how to use it. I can gut you in three seconds flat."

His brow wrinkled. "That's not an image I want to examine too closely." He took the wine she offered and sipped it with all the elegance of a titled nobleman. His gaze dipped to her attire, but he lifted it again quickly.

They watched each other in silence, both sipping wine. Finally, she sat on the edge of her bed, tucking her bare feet under her robe. Her knife was beside her.

"It's been a long time, Kate," Henry said when his glass was half empty. "I thought I'd never see you again."

"I'm sure you wish you hadn't."

"This isn't how I would have chosen to renew our acquaintance."

She gave a short laugh. "If you'd known what I'd become, you wouldn't want to be acquainted with me at all. I'm not suitable company for a viscount."

His face wrinkled in annoyance. "You think I'd put title above our friendship?"

"I don't know," she said slowly. "I don't know Viscount Bexley. The Henry I knew didn't scurry about to do the prince's bidding, didn't strut through Vauxhall giving orders, didn't dress as though he were a peacock."

She gave a pointed look to his tight coat and crisp white cravat—at least it had been crisp and white.

"The Kate Dunn I knew didn't assault innocent men or threaten them with knives, not to mention abducting them."

"We've both changed," she admitted.

"What happened?" he asked, moving closer to her. She stiffened and held up a hand, a clear warning for him to stay back. He nodded. "One day I saw you, and the next you had disappeared. You never even said good-bye."

Her heart constricted, and she clenched her hands. She could not allow him to wiggle through her defenses. She wasn't Kate Dunn anymore, and he wasn't Henry Selkirk. "I'm certain my disappearance warranted a quarter hour of discussion over dinner, if that. But don't pretend you actually missed me, my lord. Don't pretend you looked for me."

She'd wanted him to look for her, wanted him to find her, to save her. But he'd never come. No one had come.

She'd had to save herself.

"I did look for you. I inquired—"

"Stop." She waved his paltry words away. "We were children. Life happened *to* us. We're not children any longer. We shape our lives and our future."

He sipped his wine again, regarding her over the rim of the glass. Those eyes. She had to look away from those eyes. They looked through her, penetrated her defenses. They always had.

"What are you saying?" His voice was flat.

"You are a problem for me, Lord Bexley."

"After all we shared, that's the sum of what I am to you?"

She jumped to her feet. "If you meant nothing to me, you wouldn't be standing here. You wouldn't be alive."

"You're a murderess now?"

"I'm worse than that. I am every ill Society has ever conceived of. Think of the worst hovel you can imagine; I lived there. Think of the worst crime ever committed; I did it. I am the Duke of Vauxhall. If you haven't heard of me, you haven't been paying attention."

She could tell by his expression he had heard of her, and even though all the evidence of who she was now had been right before him, he was only now piecing it together.

He took a step back.

"I can't think you are as bad as they say, Kate. I *know* you."

"Not anymore you don't." She advanced on him. "I will kill you, Bexley. I may not want to, but I've sinned more times than I can count. I'm damned to hell, so what's one more black mark on my soul?"

He set the empty wine glass on the bedside table. "What do you want from me?"

Finally, the heart of the matter.

"Walk away. From the prince and from Vauxhall. Your…shall we call them improvements are cutting into my profits. More constables make it harder for my cubs to pick pockets. More lights make it difficult for my gang to sneak in and out of the gardens. And now that Barrett has all of your meaningless assurances of safety, he isn't paying his insurance."

Henry's brows rose. "Is that what you call extortion in your circle?"

"I don't have a circle, Bexley," she said, advancing on him until she was all but touching him. He was a head taller than she, but she didn't allow his height to intimidate her. "I have a band of malefactors and miscreants, and you do not want me to give them free rein."

He folded his arms, the action causing him to brush against her. "If all you needed to do was issue them free rein, then why abduct me?"

Oh, Henry was no fool. He never had been.

"I'm not a savage, Bexley. I'd like to accomplish my goals without bloodshed or violence. Besides, if the public is scared away from Vauxhall Gardens, the prince's celebration will be poorly attended. That isn't good for business either."

"So if I understand correctly, you want me to resign my position with the prince and run back home with my tail between my legs."

She shrugged. "Go home however you wish. I seem to remember you arriving in a coach and four."

"You've been watching me," he said, and for whatever reason, the tone of his voice made her breath catch.

"I like to know my adversary."

"I'd expect nothing less. And if you've been watching me, you know I don't take this position lightly. You might even know that it wasn't of my choosing."

"Are your knees rough from all the bootlicking?" she asked sarcastically. "My own have calluses, I assure you. But I don't lick…boots anymore."

Quite suddenly, he put a hand on her shoulder. She reached for her dagger, but it wasn't at her side. She'd left it on the bed. Careless and stupid of her.

"Don't touch me," she said.

"Why? Afraid you'll feel human again for a moment or two? You've explained your position, Kate. Now hear mine." His hand seemed to burn through the thin silk of her robe, straight into her cold flesh. It had been so long since she'd been touched, and she couldn't remember the last time a man had touched her gently and without anger.

But that was a lie, because the last man to touch her that way was the same one touching her now.

Henry's hand sat heavy on her shoulder. But he didn't grip her. She could have shrugged him off. To her shame, she didn't.

"I may not have wanted this title," he said. "But it's mine. I may not have wanted to serve the prince in this capacity, but I see it as serving my country. And your threats, stark as they are, won't sway me from doing my duty."

"They are not mere threats, sir," she hissed. Now she did shrug his hand from her shoulder and moved back toward the bed. "And we are at an impasse."

She knew him well enough to know he would never shirk his duty. It was one of the reasons she'd always loved him. He did what he thought was right and damn the consequences. Damn him. He would force her to kill him. She reached back and slipped the knife into her sleeve.

"Not an impasse," he said.

She arched her brow.

"What if I told you I could make this mutually beneficial for everyone?"

"I'd say you belong in Bedlam." The knife was cold in her hand, hard and cold.

"I'm not insane."

"Then you're lying."

He frowned at her. "You know me better than that. Won't you even give me a chance?"

"I don't trust you," she said.

"But you would have trusted me enough to let me go had I agreed to resign. Give me the opportunity to find a solution that's mutually beneficial. Not every outcome must favor only one party." He reached up and stroked her cheek.

At his touch, Kate snapped. It was one thing for him to touch her shoulder, but touching her like this, like a lover, was unpardonable. She flicked the dagger out from her sleeve and held it under his chin. His hand stilled, and his gaze locked on hers.

"I told you not to touch me." She moved in a circle, forcing him to move with her.

"Why not?"

"I don't like it." They'd traded places now, and his back was to the bed.

"Are you certain? Perhaps you're afraid you'll like it too much."

She shoved him back hard with a hand to his sternum. He fell back, not attempting to resist her at all. She crouched over him, her knife poised over his heart.

"Perhaps you want to die today."

He gave her a half smile. "It would save me some trouble."

Kate wanted to hit him. Why did he smile at her? Why wasn't he afraid? Why wasn't he begging for his life? He wasn't even trembling, and she was forced to award him grudging admiration. Didn't he think she would kill him? She would. She saw where his pulse beat evenly in his neck. She could cut him there, end him forever.

"Kate, I know you don't trust me anymore, but you trusted me once. Give me a chance now. Let me prove to you that I can find a solution we'll both agree upon."

Trust him? Everyone she had ever trusted had betrayed her. She'd learned early that if she didn't trust, she didn't get hurt. But he was right. She had trusted him, and though she considered his abandonment a betrayal, she knew it an unreasonable expectation. He was only two years older than she, and when they'd last seen each other, she'd barely been twelve. He couldn't have helped her even if he'd wanted to. Generally, she didn't care about fairness, but perhaps in this case she could admit her judgment of him unwarranted.

"How do I know you won't betray me?" she asked.

"How do I know you won't order me killed?" he countered.

"You don't."

He inclined his head slightly. She considered.

After a long silence, he said, "This isn't any easier for me than you. My own trust has been violated in the past, and not even the distant past."

"Somehow, I think our situations are not quite equivalent."

"Yes, you don't have a knife pointed at your heart."

She looked down at the dagger. She could kill him. She could finish this now. The Duke of Vauxhall didn't trust noblemen. She didn't trust anyone.

Squeezing the handle of the dagger, she shoved it down and into his flesh. His eyes widened in disbelief, and his hands came up to grip hers. And then he frowned.

Because he wasn't in pain. He wasn't bleeding. He wasn't dead.

His hands slipped to her wrists, and she lifted the dagger, showing him the false blade, then flipping it to the real blade. "Next time I'll use this side, and if you betray me, I'll make certain you suffer."

He sat, pushing her off him and to the side. Brushing at his shoulders, he stood, as though he had been the one in control all along. "Charming to the last," he murmured. "Where is my man? The sooner I leave, the sooner we can both get on with the business of never seeing each other again."

"Red!" she called, going to the door when the quick answer came from the other side.

"Duke, right here."

She opened the door, and Red's eyes flicked to Bexley before they went back to her. She couldn't always read Red, but tonight she saw surprise in his face. He'd expected her to kill Bexley. She would probably regret not having done it. "Bring the viscount's man out and take him and Lord Bexley back to Vauxhall."

"Yes, Duke."

"Allow them to leave unmolested. But Red"—she looked over her shoulder at Bexley—"if he gives you any trouble, leave him bleeding in a ditch on the side of the road."

"Gladly, Duke." Red pointed a finger to Bexley. "You, let's go."

Henry walked past her, his gaze forward. When his shoulder almost grazed hers, he moved it to avoid touching her. She stood in the open doorway, but he never looked back.

Chapter Three

If Henry judged by the crush of bodies, the masquerade held in the Grove was a resounding success. All of London—and a sizable portion of the other cities in England—had come to Vauxhall for the first night of celebrations in honor of the prince and Wellington's victory over Napoleon.

The night was in its infancy, which meant the masquerade was still tame. Women wore the garb of ancient goddesses, shepherdesses, and milkmaids. Others dressed as brightly plumed birds or lushly attired lions and tigers. The men were more staid in their dominoes and masks. Some had dressed as heroic warriors of the past or political figures of the present, but most, like Henry, had worn a coat and breeches and donned a simple mask.

"Splendid," Prinny said, slapping Henry on the shoulder. Henry glanced at the Prince Regent, whose face was brightly rouged and accented with a black beauty mark on one cheek. The prince had come as Zeus, the Greek god of Olympus. Henry didn't know where the man had found so much gold fabric. There must have been yards and yards of it encompassing the prince's large figure.

145

"Your costume is brilliant, Your Highness," Henry said.

The prince preened. "Do you think so? Skiffy had it made for me."

That explained quite a lot.

"Do you think it too risqué?" the prince whispered loudly. "Is it too shocking that I show my legs?"

Henry had studiously avoided looking at the prince's pale and skinny legs. He might have preferred the prince dress more like his brothers, Cumberland and York who dressed as a knight and a gladiator, but Henry supposed it could have been worse. "It is a bold statement, Your Highness."

The prince smiled, drinking in the flattery as he always did. "And you managed to do all of this on that meager budget you proposed?" he asked, extending his hand over the crowd of dancers.

"Yes, Your Highness."

"But there will be fireworks later?"

"Of course, sir."

"And we will not run out of champagne?"

"No." At least, the prince would not. The rest of the guests had been given one drink ticket with the cost of admission. If they wanted additional glasses of champagne, they had to pay. Henry had expected more grumbling at the cost of a ticket to the masked ball, but despite the high price, people had eagerly paid it. It seemed to him that the more it cost, the more people clamored to attend.

The prince cared nothing for those details. He cared only that his ball was a crush and that the food and drink flowed freely.

"If you'll excuse me, Your Highness, I have matters to attend to."

"Always working, aren't you, Bexley? Have a little fun!"

"Yes, Your Highness."

The prince sighed when Henry didn't immediately begin drinking or dancing and waved him away, turning to his friend Baron Alvanley.

Henry did not run in the other direction, not precisely, but he could not disguise his relief at having that part of the evening over and done. He'd have to speak with the prince again later this evening, but he would not think of that now.

Now he had more pressing concerns.

And the biggest of those was a criminal called the Duke of Vauxhall. He still couldn't quite believe that little Kate Dunn was the notorious Duke of Vauxhall. Henry had read about the notorious rogue. Everyone from the Mayor of London to the Bow Street Runners had called for his apprehension. Of course, what they didn't know was that the Duke of Vauxhall wasn't a man at all. That was how Kate had managed to evade detection this long. No one was looking for a young woman, and Henry imagined she could switch disguises quickly if it became necessary.

What amazed him was that her men had kept her secret. It was possible some of the newer members of the gang did not know she was a woman. After all, the disguise had fooled him. But it wouldn't have fooled him for long. Any close inspection of her face or the way her bottom was just a bit too curvy in her trousers would reveal who she really was. Her gang was either intensely loyal or too terrified to snitch on her.

Perhaps both.

It was difficult for him not to admire someone who had come from so little and accomplished so much—even if what was accomplished was more likely to see her hanged than praised. He would have never thought Kate Dunn capable of becoming a crime lord. Not because he didn't think her clever. She'd always been clever and knowledgeable. She'd had a scattered education at best, but she'd read more than anyone he knew and had an interest in anything and everything.

When they'd been small children—he six and she four—their families had lived next door to each other. His father was a solicitor for the wealthy families of Mayfair. He dealt with banks and money and contracts all day long. He knew what he was about, having grown up as the nephew of a viscount. Initially, her father had also owned a respectable business, a watch-repair shop. He was a man born with the ability to look at a broken watch and know immediately what ailed it. The work was meticulous and required focus, and as the years passed, George Dunn had spent more time at the tavern and less time in his shop. When he was at work, he was often ill from overindulgence. With his hands shaking and his skin white and clammy, his work suffered. His patrons did not return.

When his shop closed and the Dunn family moved to cheaper lodgings—the beginning of her family's downward slide into poverty and disrepute—Henry and Kate remained friends. She would visit Henry almost daily.

Henry had often wished she were a boy. If she'd been a boy, his father might have taken her in. But she was a girl, and a pretty girl at that. The poorer her family became, the less his father approved of Henry's friendship with Kate. But of course, by the time his father forbade him to see Kate, Henry was already in love with her.

Surely she'd felt something too. Perhaps she still felt something, else she wouldn't have spared him when she could have easily killed him. But Henry remembered Hedgehog and the sickening thud of metal against flesh and bone, and he would take no chances.

Henry nodded at the two constables who now flanked him whenever he went out, and the three of them moved away from the prince and his cronies and to another box, where Henry might observe the ball. These boxes, raised platforms that were covered, had sold for an additional sum. It offered those who had the funds a place to sit and watch the masque between dances. Of course, patrons could always purchase one of the supper boxes that lined three sides of the Grove, but these new boxes were more ornate and offered better prospects. Henry had reserved this one for himself. The prince's box had the best view of the dancing, but Henry had a clear view from this box as well.

The constables stood behind him, blocking the doorway, while Henry stood, hands on hips, to watch the dance. The night might be barely toddling along, but already Henry spotted men taking small liberties and ladies allowing them. Anonymity seemed to relax the rules and strictures. Henry wasn't really paying attention to the dancers. His interest lay in whether the constables were stationed where they ought to be and whether the servers returned quickly with glasses of wine and punch. He'd determined that everything seemed to be operating just as he wanted when a young girl all in white caught his eye. She wore a gold mask and a gold coronet over a long cascade of dark curls. Her dress was Greek in style, leaving her arms and shoulders bare. Gold braiding twined about the woman's waist, accentuating its slenderness, and crisscrossed her chest, drawing attention to her small but round bosom. She was small and delicate, accompanied by a larger man wearing a mask and domino that completely concealed his face and all but the very back of his hair.

As she moved through the crowd, men stopped her to exchange a word or two. She smiled up at them, her teeth white against the red of her lips. She spoke with one man now. His gaze was intent upon her, and Henry happened to wonder what her partner thought of the attention she garnered. He glanced at the man in the domino just as he reached into the pocket of the man speaking to the lovely woman. When he had the other man's purse under his domino and out of view, he put his hand on the lady's elbow and they moved on.

Henry felt ice slide down his back. It was Kate. It had to be. And the man with her—Henry narrowed his eyes and caught the flash of ginger hair—was Red.

Henry shouldn't have been surprised she was here. He supposed it was too much to hope that she'd leave Vauxhall to him for the duration of the celebration. But when she hadn't answered the letters he'd sent to her at The Griffin and the Unicorn, he'd thought perhaps she had reconsidered. Now he began to worry she hadn't received the letters, which meant she would be looking to punish him for lying to her.

He flexed his fingers. He liked them all in one piece.

Clearly, the cautious thing to do—the safe thing—would be to stay here with his constables where he was protected. Of course, that was also the cowardly thing. Not to mention the irresponsible thing. In the time since he'd spotted her, she and her partner had stolen from three more men. At this rate, all of his guests would be complaining about being robbed. That certainly wouldn't show the prince and his celebration in the best light. Henry glanced about for his constables. Why didn't they stop the little thief?

But though they were watching, their gazes sharp, it seemed they either looked past Kate or their gazes lingered on her figure, not on the man taking advantage of her charm and beauty to rob the guests—*Henry's* guests—blind.

"Bloody hell." Henry turned and started for the door.

"Should we follow, my lord?" one of his private constables asked.

"Yes, and be ready. We must apprehend a thief."

"Yes, my lord!"

Henry walked quickly and with purpose to the edge of the dance floor. Of course, when he reached the last location he'd seen her, she wasn't there any longer. But he soon spotted the long curls threaded with gold. It must have been a wig, but it was an expensive one. It looked real enough, especially as he neared and saw it in more detail. Before he could reach out to touch her arm, Red stepped in front of him.

"Step back, sir. She is with me."

Henry raised his mask. "I think you are the one who had better step back. As of right now, you are both with *me*." He jerked his head toward his men, who moved forward. But just then Kate whirled and gave him a bright smile. Henry blinked and had to remind himself to breathe. She obviously had a similar effect on his constables, because they stopped midstep.

"Lord Bexley," Kate said sweetly, her accent distinctly upper class. "How lovely to see you again."

Henry inclined his head. "And you, Miss Dunn. I'd like to speak to you in private."

"Would you?" Her smiled remained fixed in place, but her dark eyes were hard and cold. He was right to think she would be angry with him. She was furious. If she had any iron bars within reach, he was done for.

"I think there might be a misunderstanding," he said.

"Is that what you are calling it?" She lifted her hand and made a shooing motion. "By all means, lead the way. I find I have a few words for you as well, my lord."

He offered her his arm, because it was the correct thing to do and because he didn't trust her not to stab him in the back. His constables flanked Red, and the five of them started away. But as soon as Kate realized they were headed for the boxes, she drew back. "No, not private enough, and I don't like to be boxed in." She smiled. Kate and her bad puns.

"I'm not sure exactly *how* private I want to be with you, Miss Dunn," Henry said.

"Then you shall have to trust me when I say we will want to be *very* private indeed, my lord." She whispered the words, her tone teasing and full of promise. To his annoyance, Henry felt himself go hard. His body reacted to her, even though his mind knew she would rather slit his throat than allow him to kiss her.

And in spite of what he knew about her, what he'd learned about her, he did want to kiss her. The problem was that he'd kissed her before—years ago, true—and he'd never forgotten those kisses.

"Where would you suggest, Miss Dunn?" he asked.

"I know a grotto not far from here. I would think it deserted this early in the evening. If it's not, then Red will speak with the occupants on our behalf."

Henry glanced over his shoulder at her thug. "Yes, I'm sure he will." He allowed her to lead the way, and though she led him into a part of the gardens with which he was unfamiliar, it was not so far from the ball that he worried he would be lost or would not be heard should he need assistance. The grotto was in shadow, but the nearby lamps shed some light. It was also empty, the cave being shallow enough that he could see inside to where an iron bench sat beside a small waterfall.

"Shall we?" she asked, indicating the grotto. "Your…friends may wait out here with Red. We can choose to be in full view the entire time."

Choose to be in full view… Did that mean the grotto curved back so that a portion of it was shielded from passersby? Knowing Vauxhall as he did, Henry suspected that was the case. He tried not to ignore the way his heart pounded harder at the thought of being alone with Kate, out of view, and her in the thin white costume.

He followed her into the grotto, sitting beside her when she situated herself on the bench. The waterfall behind them was small enough that they didn't have to raise their voices to be heard, but it would muffle their words and keep sound from carrying.

Kate turned to him as soon as he sat. "Do you know how close to death you are?"

"Can't you ever begin a conversation in the usual fashion? *Hello, Henry. How are you? How are your parents? What do you think of this lovely summer weather?*"

"I don't care about the weather or your parents. I trusted you, and you betrayed me." She carried a small white reticule with gold braided tassels, and now she reached inside and caught hold of the hilt of a knife. Henry doubted this one would retract upon impact.

"Don't be so hasty." He clamped a hand on her wrist and held it tightly, keeping her from withdrawing the knife from the bag. "I think you owe me an explanation. I didn't betray your trust. I did just as I said I would."

"You hired more pigs. The place is crawling with constables, watchmen, and Runners."

"Not that it stopped you. You must have made a nice profit in the quarter hour I saw you."

"I could have made twenty times that if half my cubs hadn't been caught and tossed in the stone doublet for a fortnight."

Prison. Her gang was short on members, and that was why she was picking pockets herself. "Then you didn't take my advice."

"What advice?" she asked between clenched teeth.

"The advice I included in the letters I sent."

Her hand, so tense and stiff, relaxed slightly. "What letters?"

With the immediate danger to his life slightly less, he couldn't help but lower his gaze to the curve of her bare shoulder. Her skin was so pale it

154 | Shana Galen

was nearly translucent. It looked soft and sleek, and if her small wrist in his hand was any indication, it was all of that and more.

"My eyes are up here, Lord Bexley."

He looked into her dark eyes, which weren't quite so hard as before. "Forgive me. I'd forgotten how pretty you are."

She rolled her eyes. "The hair, the cosmetics, the dress—it's all an illusion meant to distract foolish men like you."

"I was not looking at your hair or your cosmetics. I like your real hair much better than that profusion of curls, and you certainly don't need cosmetics. Your skin is already perfect."

"If you think flattery will save you—"

"You know me better than that, Kate."

She closed her mouth, and he thanked God she really did know he was not one for false compliments. But he was having a very hard time not sliding his gaze to her cleavage. The way her breasts pushed against the material of the gown made him wonder if she wore any undergarments beneath it.

"We were speaking of letters," she said. "I never received any letters."

"Are you still at The Griffin and the Unicorn?"

"I can be reached there," she said with a note of caution that he admired.

"I sent the letters there, addressed to His Grace, the Duke of V."

She shook her head. "I didn't receive them." Then, to his surprise, she looked away. "I didn't expect you to send a letter."

"How did you think I would communicate?"

"I…" She bit her lip. "I made a mistake." She looked back at him, her eyes hard again. "I admit it."

"I very much doubt it happens often," he said.

"Why do you say that?"

"Because you're still alive. After all these years, I didn't think I'd see you again."

Her gaze met his, the warm brown eyes the same as he remembered all those years ago. He couldn't help but look at her mouth and remember the kisses they'd shared then. They'd been little more than children and the kisses quite innocent, but he'd never forgotten the feel of her soft lips and the press of her sweet mouth against his. He wondered if she felt the same, and as if in response, she lifted her arm and wrapped a hand around the back of his neck, cupping it. He didn't resist, and his mouth slowly lowered to hers.

"Duke, there's someone coming." The hissed words were like ice sliding between them. Kate released him.

Her eyes had turned hard again. "One of your constables?"

Henry blew out a breath. And he had thought he was overly cautious. "No one knows I'm with you except the two men out there with your man. It's probably just stragglers from the ball."

"He wouldn't have called out if it was only revelers." She grasped Henry's arm and pulled him back into the shadows. To Henry's surprise, the grotto extended farther back than he'd expected. The passage became dark and narrow, but there was enough room for the two of them if they pressed together.

That was when Henry knew Kate was not wearing any stays under her gown. He doubted she even wore a chemise. The stone around them was cold, and he could feel the hard points of her nipples straining against the thin fabric of her costume.

"You're enjoying this," she said. Tangled together as they were, he could not hide his arousal.

"Pure physical response," he said. "I can't control it."

"Does this happen every time you're near a woman?"

"No." In fact, he was usually much better at controlling his body and his desires. "But I admit I have been remembering kissing you since I first realized who you are."

"I've thought of those kisses too." Her low voice seemed to brush over him like velvet. He slid, his hands over her hips to envelope her and pull her closer.

"Probably safer if we only remember them."

"Sometimes I don't like to play safe." Her arms went around his neck, and her soft breasts pressed against his chest.

"Kiss me," he said, the words half demand, half plea. He would have kissed her, but he hadn't forgotten the knife in her reticule, and he didn't want to end the night with a dagger protruding from his neck.

She pulled him closer and, rising on tiptoe, locked her mouth with his.

Chapter Four

The kiss was everything she'd hoped and more. She brushed her mouth over his, and that seemed all he needed to respond wholeheartedly. His mouth slid over hers in a way both familiar and novel. His lips were smooth and skilled, his mouth teasing her with sensual promises. She remembered the thrill of his tongue touching hers when they'd been young and in love. Now when she opened her mouth and his tongue invaded, everything was the same and also wonderfully different. He'd kissed other women, and quite a few, that much was clear. He knew what to do to make her hand fist in his hair and a sigh followed by a low moan escape her lips.

But she had kissed her share of men. None had ever kissed her this tenderly, but she was not wholly without ammunition. And she wanted to slay him. She wanted him to feel as dizzy and hot and needy as she did.

And so she met his tongue thrust for thrust, deepening the kiss, moving closer, taking all he had and giving it right back. His hands tightened on her waist, and he pushed her back against the cold, hard rock. His leg parted her thighs, and she felt the warmth of his knee between her legs. Given another minute, she might have been carried away enough to press back against his knee and relieve some of the tension coiling in her sex. Instead, she drew back and slowly broke the kiss.

She was the Duke of Vauxhall first and Kate Dunn second. The kiss had been for Kate—a momentary lapse of judgment. Now the duke was back, and she had business.

"Kate," Henry whispered, his voice ragged and so full of heat it almost undid her. Instead of drawing him back to her, as she wanted, she pushed him and stepped away from the rough wall.

"Nice to know my memories were accurate," she said.

He gave a short laugh. "Mine were sorely lacking." He pulled her back into his arms. "Kiss me again. I can't get enough of you."

She put a hand on his chest, and that was all it took. His hands dropped, and he stepped back. She was momentarily stunned at how easily he had acquiesced to her wishes, but then she did not surround herself with men who knew anything about respecting women. Henry's father had never been anything but respectful of his wife, and he'd taught Henry to be the same. It was the reason Henry had never done more than kiss Kate, though he'd been older and could have easily taken advantage of her. Henry might have wanted to touch her budding breasts or feel under her skirts, but he'd always kept his hands firmly on her shoulders when they'd kissed.

She gave a brief whistle, imitating the sound of an owl. A moment later, she had her reply. The unwelcome guests had moved on. Kate scooted along the wall of the grotto until a beam of light once again penetrated the darkness. She did not go out into the open. She didn't want Red to see much more than a glimpse of her so he would know she was well.

"You said something about letters," she said to Henry when she had her breath back.

He moved closer to the light as well, and in the semidark, she saw him nod. "I suppose most of your gang can't read."

"A few can, and if they'd known to look for letters, they would have brought any that came to me. As it is, your notes were probably used to wipe someone's arse."

"Lovely."

"Tell me what they said."

"They said I have a proposition for you."

"I'm assuming the proposition was not that you would retire as Prinny's lackey and withdraw the additional constables."

"The security measures are inevitable, Kate, whether you deal with me or another man."

"I think you forget how persuasive I can be."

He gave her a wry look. "You can't kill us all, and with that in mind, I suggest you join us."

Her hand was around the knife hilt again before she could stop herself. "I should have killed you at The Griffin and the Unicorn."

He held up a hand. "Far too messy."

"Not as messy as trying to hide a body in Vauxhall Gardens."

"Before you make any unfortunate decisions, hear me out. I promised a solution that is mutually beneficial. I need servers and lodgings. I could use your men to serve guests at the forthcoming events, and I would happily recommend The Griffin and the Unicorn as the prince's choice lodgings in Lambeth."

"The prince has never been to The Griffin and the Unicorn."

"That doesn't matter. It's the association with his name that matters."

"And why would I give you men to serve wine and thinly sliced ham to rich nobs? How does that benefit me?"

"You want blunt. That's why you're picking pockets. I'll pay you."

She laughed and shook her head. "Honest work? I've tried it and I nearly starved. I can make more begging on the street." She had heard enough. She started away, too disgusted to even gut him as she should.

"I'll pay your men fairly, and what they lose in profits as servers, you will make up with the crowds I'll send to The Griffin and the Unicorn."

Kate paused. "Crowds?"

"The Griffin and the Unicorn makes a convenient flash ken for your gang, but did you ever think about legitimizing it? The location is ideal. You could fill the public room and all the bedchambers every night Vauxhall is open."

"That's only three nights a week."

He spread his hands. "But you can make up for your losses on the other four days with the overflow of revelers during the prince's celebration. Think about it, Kate. The inn has untapped potential."

She was thinking about it, and she was thinking she'd been a fool never to have considered taking this route before. Not assisting Henry with serving at the gardens—that was a losing proposition. Her cubs would end up causing trouble or forget not to pick pockets, and that would be the end of that. But managing an inn... She had enough people. They only needed direction. Vauxhall would close for several days after tonight. In that time, the inn could be made ready for dozens of guests and the public room rearranged to accommodate more guests as well.

"You like the idea," he said, his gaze on her face. She didn't like that he could read her so easily, but then, she'd lowered her guard with him.

"I'm thinking it over."

"Why don't I give you an extra incentive?"

Her eyes narrowed. "Why?"

"Because we're old friends."

She raised one brow.

He sighed. "Because I very much want you to consider suspending your criminal activities in Vauxhall until after the prince's celebrations."

"And if I don't?"

"Lovely Kate," he said with a conciliatory smile. "Charming Kate. I like how you consider all the different outcomes. For now, let's focus on one. Will you consider my proposition?"

"I'll consider it."

"Good. Then factor this in as well. If you agree to it, I will do all I can to ensure The Griffin and the Unicorn is a success."

"That's the incentive?"

"Part of it. The other part is you will work closely with me."

She almost smiled. Instead, she crossed her arms. "How is that an incentive?"

"Give me a chance, and I'll show you," he said. He might call her charming, but he was the charming one. She could hardly resist him.

"Come to the inn tomorrow afternoon. We'll discuss it further."

"Tomorrow? I—"

She cut him off with a finger to his lips. She wasn't wearing gloves— men were easily distracted by bare arms—and his mouth felt warm under her fingertip. "Lord Bexley, I am the Duke of Vauxhall. When I call, you come." And damn his other plans. She wouldn't be put off so he could sip tea at a garden party or some such nonsense.

"I'll be there."

She lifted her finger. "This had better not be a waste of my time."

"If it is, you can always slit my throat."

"I'd already planned to," she said, turning away to hide her smile at the horrified look on his face. She wouldn't slit his throat. She wanted him to kiss her again too much.

But if he betrayed her, then even his persuasive lips would not save him. She'd do much worse than slit his throat.

***

Henry sometimes wondered how he managed to get himself into these sorts of messes. He wondered that upon strolling into the public room of The Griffin and the Unicorn and facing three thugs with wicked daggers drawn.

"Good day," he said, trying to control the tremor in his voice. "I believe the duke is expecting me."

The blond he remembered from the first night when he'd been abducted lowered his knife. He didn't sheathe it, but he pointed it toward Henry's foot rather than his heart, which was somewhat reassuring. "I'll see if the duke is ready for you," he said.

That left Henry alone with the other two thugs, who did not lower their knives or so much as offer him a seat. He stood, shifting uneasily, for what seemed quite a long time. But then the minutes did drag when one's life was hanging in the balance.

This was the first time Henry had been held at knifepoint by thugs (if he did not include the incident with Kate in her bedchamber), but not the first time he'd wished his life had taken a different path. No one had held a knife to his throat when he'd become a viscount, but they might as well have. He'd had about as much choice in that matter as he did with the actual blades before him. He'd never wanted the title or the responsibility. Henry had wanted to become a barrister. He'd gone to school and opened a little office with a school chum of his. The two of them had starved and frozen, but they'd begun to gain traction—mostly by taking the cases no one else wanted—when his father died.

It seemed Henry had hardly recovered from that blow when his cousin was done in by the careless riding, and before Henry knew which end was up, people were addressing him as Lord Bexley and shoving him into Parliament. He was responsible for estates he had never seen, tenants he had never met, and a fortune he had never anticipated. Though as to that fortune, the account books were so tangled and the entries so haphazard, he was not certain whether he was rich or in debt up to his eyebrows. There was much he could and should have been doing these past months. Instead, he'd been forced to call on the Prince Regent almost daily in order to convince the mercurial prince that adding to his plans or embellishing them was not truly in his or the country's best interest.

And now, on a day when the prince was likely still abed and suffering from the effects of too much indulgence, Henry was not at his desk, scratching his head over illegible ledgers, but standing in the public room of a shabby inn with knives pointed at his heart.

Idly, he surveyed the room, noting small changes here and there that would enliven the place and make it look newer and more fashionable. Kate had never been one to notice fashion. As a girl, she hadn't seemed to care about the latest dress styles or coiffures. Henry had always thought that was mostly because she could not afford the expense associated with the latest fashions. She had not been the sort to covet or whine about her misfortunes, so she'd simply ignored what was beyond her reach.

Henry thought he could be of some use in suggesting minor changes to the inn—for example, doing away with the knife-wielding thugs who greeted patrons. That was if she was receptive to his suggestions. Which seemed unlikely, considering she had seen fit to make him wait the past quarter hour.

Or perhaps she was busy with a previous engagement. She might have more hands to smash.

Or a lover in her bed.

Henry did not know where that thought came from, and he liked even less the reaction he felt. He wasn't a jealous man, but then, Kate was different. She'd always been different. She was the only female he'd ever been friends with. The first girl he'd kissed. The first girl—the only female—he'd ever loved.

But that was before. They'd been children. Now, he was Viscount Bexley and she was a criminal. Despite the kiss they'd shared—a kiss he thought about far more often than he should—their positions in Society made any relationship between them impossible.

Their association now was based completely on mutual self-interest. He would keep the criminal element away from Vauxhall during the prince's celebrations, and she would make a profit. The kiss had not been a part of that arrangement. It had been nothing more than a remnant of the past. Now that they'd relived the past, they could put it aside. They were both very different people now.

The blond man returned and cocked his head toward the door. "Duke will see you."

Henry would have felt relief at being led away from the knife-wielding thugs, but he was most likely walking into a far more dangerous situation.

He was led into her library. Henry wasn't certain if that was how she thought of it. Perhaps she considered it her torture chamber, as it was the same room where she'd smashed Hedgehog's hand. But it had books and armchairs and a thick rug, and so in Henry's mind, he referred to it as the library.

The blond tapped once then opened the door. With a shove, Henry was thrust inside.

Henry stumbled then recovered, brushing at his sleeves and coat to right himself. "That was unnecessary," he muttered.

"Don't expect civility here," came the familiar low, velvet voice. "You won't find it. Drink?"

She was seated at the desk where she'd ruined Hedgehog's hand. She sat sideways, legs looped over one arm of the chair, watching him. She was dressed as a man again—trousers, linen shirt, coat—but she didn't wear her hat. Henry doubted any man who looked at her lovely skin, her dark eyes, or her pink lips would be fooled into thinking she was a man.

She gestured to a crystal decanter filled with an amber liquid. Brandy, Henry thought. He could have used a sip, but he wanted his wits unimpaired.

"No, thank you."

"Coffee, then?" she asked. She held up a small china cup. "It's what I'm having."

"Very well."

"Serve yourself," she told him, making no attempt to adhere to any social graces. Henry didn't mind. There wasn't any artifice with her. He liked knowing she didn't play a part. When he'd poured the coffee into a cup matching hers, he took the seat across from her.

"I have some ideas for how you might drum up revenue at The Griffin and the Unicorn," he said.

"Do you?" She arched a brow. "I wasn't aware I'd accepted your proposal."

Henry set down the cup he'd been about to sip from. "If you aren't interested, then why did you insist I come today?"

"To discuss our options. I thought I was clear on that point, but perhaps our kiss muddled your brain."

Henry clenched his jaw. "Perhaps it muddled yours," he said tightly.

"Not at all. I've thought about your proposition. I think we could make a profit if we spruced up the inn and if you do your part to bolster its reputation."

"Good. With that income and the wages your men will earn as servers—"

"My men will not serve at Vauxhall. I told you. That won't work."

"Then I can't be responsible for that portion of the lost revenue."

She kicked her legs down and swiveled to face him, her hands resting on the desk. "Oh, you are responsible for it, and you'll help me, or I'll make certain Prinny's little fete is a complete and utter disaster."

"You are welcome to try."

"I won't have to try very hard. One or two small incidents will be more than enough to taint the public's view and ruin you."

She was right. Of course she was right. But perhaps ruination was preferable to negotiating with a crime lord.

"I don't want to ruin you, Lord Bexley," she said quietly. "You've always been my friend, and I believe you're still my friend. Are you my friend?"

"The question, Kate, is are you mine?"

"I want to be. I want to believe the boy I knew is somewhere inside the coat from Weston and the boots from Hoby."

He began to rise. "If last night didn't show you—"

"All I want is for you to get into bed with me," she interrupted.

Henry sat back down. "Could you say that again?"

She smiled. "*Get into bed with me*. It's a saying, Henry. Like *row in my boat*. I want you on my side."

"I am on your side."

"Then prove it."

He made a sweeping gesture to encompass the room. "Here I am. This should be proof enough. If anyone ever finds out I am meeting with the Duke of Vauxhall, I'll be more than ruined. I'll be brought up on charges and have my neck stretched on the gallows."

"No one will find out. And I promise that if you help me with one more task, my men and I will confine ourselves to the inn until after the celebration is over. Vauxhall will be barren of rogues—*my* rogues, at any rate."

Henry knew he should walk away. He knew he wouldn't like what she said. But if he walked away, he'd never see her again. That seemed a fate worse than ruination, worse than the gallows even. He tried to remind himself they had no future. Their kiss the night before had been a nod to the past and nothing more.

And yet he could not stop staring at her lips and wondering if she would ever allow him to kiss her again.

"I'm listening," he said.

"Good. In two days' time, there will be a prizefight at Vauxhall, Samuel Storm versus Darius King," she said, naming two pugilists.

Henry was shaking his head. "No, there won't. I never authorized any prizefight."

"I authorized it weeks ago."

"You don't have the authority."

"I'm the bloody Duke of Vauxhall. That's all the authority I need. King is the clear favorite, but Storm is coached by Godrick Gunnery. Gunnery's name alone will bring in a pile of blunt. And who do you think receives a cut of the wagering?"

Clearly, she and her gang did, but Henry didn't for a moment believe that was the only piece of the pie she had her finger in. "And where is this fight to take place?"

"My gang will erect a tent—a large tent, mind you, such as a sheikh would have—in one of the dark walks."

Henry shook his head. "You are mad. Absolutely daft. The constables will shut it down before it even begins."

"Not if you give them the night off."

"That won't account for the Runners."

"I have a plan for them as well. Would you like to hear it?"

"No."

"Shall I tell you anyway?" She stood. "Because if my plan works, and if you help me, Vauxhall will be all yours for the rest of the season." She planted her hands on the desk and looked into his eyes, her face just inches from him.

Henry couldn't deny her anything when she was this close to him. "Tell me," he said. After all, how bad could it be?

At least, that was his logic until he heard her scheme, and then he knew he had truly made a deal with the devil.

Chapter Five

Kate didn't know why she'd never thought to enlist someone from Vauxhall before. Having Henry on her side made everything so much easier. She didn't have to climb under hedges or scale fences. She simply strolled in through the main entrance. And she didn't have to wait until it was dark on the nights the pleasure gardens were closed. She could enter during the day, just like a normal Londoner who'd come to enjoy the flowers.

Except she wasn't a normal Londoner. She was the Duke of Vauxhall, and she had much to supervise if her plan for the night of the prizefight was to be a success. And if all went as planned the night would be a spectacular victory. The Duke of Devonshire had agreed to attend and to present the winner of the fight not only a fat purse but also a ring of gold, encrusted with diamonds. Kate wanted that ring. Henry would have never agreed to that portion of her scheme, but as long as he thought all she planned was to capitalize on London's betting nature, she needn't worry. That Henry was participating at all surprised her—not that he'd agreed to participate; she'd given him little choice in the matter. The level of his participation surprised her. He was a viscount, but that didn't stop him from dirtying his hands. He put his back to the necessary manual labor along with Red, Scrugs, Davey, and all the rest. Henry dug pits, positioned ropes and nets, and obscured walking paths—and all without a word of protest.

If he hadn't already had a position in the House of Lords, she would have hired him to work for her. The first day in Vauxhall, Henry had to leave early to attend a session of the Lords. Kate had wondered how he'd managed. He'd looked exhausted when he left, and she knew the Lords could often sit for hours.

But the next day, he had arrived even before she, looking as dashing as usual with his hair neatly combed and his jaw freshly shaven.

He labored as hard as he had the day before, but she knew him well enough to see the signs of fatigue others would miss. She noted the way he rolled his neck and how often he pressed a hand to his eyes. Kate made sure to offer him extra rations of ale, scowling when she caught Red looking at her with an amused grin on his face.

"Wipe that smirk off your face," she ordered Red.

"Yes, Duke," he said and went back to shoveling excess dirt into a flowerbed where it wouldn't be seen.

After a moment, Kate put her hands on her hips. "Why were you smiling?"

Red shrugged. "I've known you a long time, Duke."

"And you're smiling because of all the times I've saved your arse?"

"Ha!" He glanced at her over his shoulder. "You mean all the times I saved *your* arse."

"If that's how you remember it, you've been hit on the head once too often." But if she was being honest, he had saved her as often as she had saved him.

"I haven't been hit so much that I don't recognize the look on your face."

"The look that says I could smash your nose with that spade at any moment?"

But Red wasn't worried. "No, this look has more to do with a lusty roll in the sheets." He inclined his head toward Henry, who was listening intently to something Scrugs was saying.

"I don't have time for rolls in the sheets," she said.

"That's too bad. This is the first time I've ever seen you interested in a man for more than what you can pick from his pocket."

"I've had my share of rolls in the sheets."

Red lowered the shovel and looked at her. "You did what you had to do. Maybe it's time you tried doing what you want to do."

She looked at him for a long time. Red didn't often speak, and he'd never offered her advice. But he did know her better and had known her longer than anyone else, save Henry. She lowered her voice. "I'm no innocent. He wouldn't want me."

"Oh, he wants you. He has the same look you do when you're not watching. And don't tell me you believe all that rubbish about men wanting a virgin. Any man worth his salt wants a wench who's clever and pretty and makes him laugh."

Kate stared at him. Was that really true? Was that the reason Henry had kissed her? Because he thought she was clever and pretty and she made him laugh? Well, she hadn't made him laugh yet, but she could. She'd thought their kiss had simply been a way to relive a moment of the past, but what if it had been more?

"So?" Red said. "What do you say?"

She put her hands on her hips again. "Did you actually call me a *wench*? Do you remember what happened to the last person who called me a *wench*?"

Red shook his head and went back to his work, closing his mouth for good this time.

But at the end of the day, when Henry didn't leave for a session of Parliament, Kate walked beside him as they exited the pleasure gardens.

"Tomorrow is the fight," Henry said, making idle conversation. "No matter what happens, you can't say I haven't done all I could to ensure success."

"We'll see what happens tomorrow."

He stopped and rounded on her. "I bloody well knew you would say that. You'll never trust me, will you?"

"I don't know. Do you claim to trust me?"

"Of course I don't trust you," he argued. "Every time I turn around, you threaten me. I never know what you'll do from one moment to the next."

Kate rather liked that description of herself. "The Lords are not sitting in Parliament tonight?" she asked.

Henry scowled at her in confusion. "No. Why should you care?"

"I don't."

He stomped away from her, and she could have kicked herself, because that was not at all what she'd meant to say. With a half-dozen quick strides, she caught up to him. "I asked because I thought you might join us at The Griffin and the Unicorn. I'm buying everyone a drink." She didn't know where that came from. She hadn't intended to do any such thing. But it was too late now. Scrugs had been walking by, and he let out a little whoop of joy. The next thing she knew, his blond head was bouncing ahead of them as he spread the news to the other men.

Since she couldn't rescind the offer now, she hoped she hadn't made it in vain. "Why don't you join us?" she suggested. "You did as much work as anyone."

Henry narrowed his eyes and looked at her for a long time. She didn't have to wonder at his thoughts. No doubt he was thinking about how to turn her down without making her so angry she slit his throat. After all, why would a viscount want to sit and drink with a gang of criminals?

"Never mind," she said, cutting him off before he could reject her. "It was a foolish idea. I'm certain you'd rather go home to your *town house* in Mayfair." She marched away, grinding her teeth against the sting of tears.

"Why would I wish to return home to an empty house?" he asked from behind her. "Don't misunderstand, I have a full complement of servants, but conversations where the other party answers nothing but *yes, my lord* and *no, my lord* do grow tiresome."

Kate found her mouth curving into a grin. "No one will be *my lording* you at The Griffin and the Unicorn." Her voice was carefully neutral.

"And you'll drink with us?"

Now she did turn so he could see her smile. "I'll give the toast."

***

Until the moment Henry sat at the bar in The Griffin and the Unicorn, he had almost convinced himself he was no longer smitten with Kate. She'd threatened him, ordered him about, and compelled him to complete her backbreaking work. When she'd asked him to have a drink with her, his one thought had been that he'd rather kill her than drink with her.

But he hadn't lied about the emptiness of his Mayfair residence. It had belonged to the Viscounts Bexley for as long as he could remember. He hadn't ever expected to live there, and after the initial awe and wonder he'd felt upon moving in and realizing the grand house was all his now, he'd wanted little more than to go back to his room above his barrister's office.

That little section of Islington was home to him. The people there were familiar. He saw the same men and women he'd seen every day since he'd been old enough to toddle out of doors. His friends were there. One or two had come to visit him in Mayfair, but everything had felt stilted and awkward and his friends hadn't returned. He was a viscount. He was supposed to make friends with earls and marquesses. But they seemed to want little to do with him. He'd been in *trade*—it was always said with a disapproving intonation—before being elevated to the rank of viscount. They might sit beside him in the Lords, but they didn't invite him to their clubs or their soirees. The one time he had thought he had made some progress and made friends, he'd been tricked into doing the other peers' dirty work.

And now he was stuck playing the disapproving banker to the Prince Regent.

Henry didn't belong at The Griffin and the Unicorn, but neither did he belong in Mayfair. He didn't know where he belonged, or where he would end up, but he knew when he was with Kate, he had the sense that he was where he should be.

In some ways, she didn't belong either. Yes, she was a celebrated lord of the underworld, but the power she held was a ruse. She dressed like a man and played the role of the Duke of Vauxhall, but she wouldn't be able to keep up the pretense forever. And when her rivals discovered she was a woman, they would come for her and her gang, and no crime lord—not even the Duke of Vauxhall—would be able to withstand that sort of attack.

The blond thug—his name was apparently Scrugs, though Henry was uncertain whether that was his given name or his surname—stood behind the bar and poured a generous measure of gin into a glass before slamming it down in front of Henry. Henry looked at the glass. He didn't usually drink gin, but he could hardly refuse without offending someone. Red and Scrugs tipped their glasses and shot theirs back, swallowing it with one gulp. Henry tried to do the same and ended up coughing for a good five minutes.

When he could breathe again, Kate was beside him. "A little strong for you, my lord?"

"No my lording," he managed to rasp out of his burning throat.

"My mistake," she said. "I have some brandy in my parlor. Would you prefer that?"

Red and Scrugs smirked at him.

"No," Henry said, clearing his throat. "Another gin, please." He pushed his glass toward Scrugs, who filled it again. Then he filled his own and tossed it back. Thirty minutes and three drinks later, the room spun and Henry was no longer tossing gin back. The gang's attention had shifted to a high-stakes dice game, and Henry was left to stare into his gin and wish he'd drunk less and stared more.

Kate pulled out the chair beside him and sat. "Sometimes I think I will never understand men," she said, staring directly in front of her. "Why do you feel the need to prove your masculinity by making yourself ill?"

"I'm not ill."

Her eyes cut to him. "Liar. You're practically green."

"I need something to soak up the alcohol."

Kate lifted a hand, and the lad behind the bar brought over a plate with bread and cheese. Henry forced himself to take a small bite of the bread.

"I worked for men," she said.

Henry stopped chewing and stared at her. She continued to look forward, not meeting his gaze. "When my mother and father were gone, I had no way to survive and so I learned to pick pockets. Eventually, I moved on to other rackets, but the one commonality was that the arch rogues were always men. So I watched them. I learned what it meant to be a man. I studied them until I knew their strengths and their weaknesses. Now I think I may be a better man than most men."

"I'm certain that would have made sense two drinks ago."

She smiled faintly. "I still have to prove myself, but I don't overimbibe because I don't have the need to protect my masculine pride."

"What about your feminine pride?" Henry asked before he could think better of it. It was better for both of them if he did not think of her as a woman. If he did not remember the way she'd looked in her bedchamber, half dressed and lovely.

"I still have my feminine pride," she said quietly. "I didn't think I did. Not until I saw you again."

Henry turned sharply, but before he could ask what she meant, she hopped off her seat. "Come have a brandy with me."

"It hurts my masculine pride to admit this, but if I drink anything else, I'll fall over."

"Then watch me drink, but a true gentleman doesn't refuse a lady his company."

He tried to hop off his stool with as much grace as she had shown, but he had to grab the bar to keep from rolling onto the floor. "I'm not much of a gentleman," he said when he'd righted himself again.

"I'm not much of a lady."

To his surprise, she took his hand and led him back to the room where he'd been brought that first night—the library/torture chamber. When they were alone inside, the door closed behind them, he looked at the desk where she'd used the iron bar so ruthlessly.

"Whatever happened to the man you called Hedgehog?"

She blew out a breath. He'd thought she would pour herself a drink. Instead, she wriggled onto the top of her desk so her trouser-clad legs hung down. "I wish you hadn't seen that."

"That makes two of us." He sat heavily on the couch. The room didn't spin as much when he sat. "But I think I understand why you did it."

"I doubt that."

"Why? Because I'm not a crime lord? We're not so different, you and I."

"Now I know you are drunk."

"Hear me out." He tried to stand—always better to make a speech standing—but thought better of it when the upward motion made his vision blur. Kate was beside him in a moment, her hand on his elbow. He shook it off and continued from where he was. "If one of my servants or my steward steals from me, I let him go without a reference. If I tolerate the theft, what's to stop others from stealing from me too? If one of your men steals from you, you have to punish him, or others will follow suit."

She raised a brow. "Smashing a man's hand is slightly different from refusing to write a letter of reference."

He shook his head and regretted the movement immediately. "Not really. You ended Hedgehog's career as a pickpocket the same way the career of a servant is ended if he or she has no reference. But here's the real question, Kate."

Her large brown eyes met his.

"Why did you stop at smashing his hand? Why didn't you kill him?"

"You want me to commit murder?"

"I want you to survive. You won't survive in your world for long if you're soft."

She gave a short bark of laughter. "You don't know anything about my world."

"I know that once your secret is out, you won't stand a chance. I can't believe you've hidden who you really are this long. What's to stop a man like Hedgehog from going to another gang and telling the—what do you call them? Arch rogues—"

She inclined her head

"—that you're a woman?"

"Nothing but fear."

"One of these days, the desire for revenge will be stronger than the fear."

She nodded slightly, as though she knew all of this. "Everyone dies. Some of us die younger than others."

"It doesn't have to be that way."

"Oh, will you sweep in and rescue me?" Her voice dripped with sarcasm. "Do you think I'm a princess in need of rescue from the fire-breathing dragon? I can save myself." She stood and paced angrily away.

"Perhaps we can save each other."

She stilled. He couldn't see her face with her back turned to him, but he knew he'd caught her attention. "You don't want this life, Kate. You're not a monster. You don't want to hurt people. If you did, you would have killed that man."

"I may yet have to kill him." She turned, and her eyes were liquid with unshed tears. "I didn't choose this life, but it's all I have. Don't pretend we can be any more to each other than we are in this room."

"And if I asked you to marry me?" He did not know if he would have said that if he hadn't been drinking, but the drink had made saying what he wanted so much easier.

"Then I'd tell you no and expect you to thank me. I no more belong in your world than you do in mine. What do you think would happen if you married me, even if no one knew I was the Duke of Vauxhall? The truth would still come out. I was a thief, a criminal, a whore."

"You'd be my wife." His voice rose now because he wanted to block out her words. None of them described the Kate he'd known or the Kate he saw standing before him now.

"I'd be an outcast, and so would you. You don't want that. If you cared nothing for your title and your duty, you wouldn't be chasing after Prinny's approval."

"I could give it up." But could he? What about his title? He hadn't wanted it, but it had existed for hundreds of years and would exist for hundreds more. Who was he to taint it? What about his family? What would they say? Could he stand strong against their censure? Against the censure of all of London? His servants would give notice, the merchants he frequented would not sell to him. In short, he would be anathema.

And he would pass his low status on to Kate and their children.

"I wouldn't ask you to give it up," Kate said, as though she could read his thoughts. "Tomorrow is the fight, and then you'll be rid of me for good." She moved closer to him. "For *good*, Henry. It's better this way."

"Funny that I can't see that at the moment."

"You will."

"No. All I see is you, Kate." He took her hands. "You're all I want to see, all I think about night and day. Even if it means digging holes in Vauxhall Gardens, I cannot wait to be with you."

"I worry about you, Henry." Her voice was soft. "If digging holes is all you have to look forward to."

He pulled her gently onto the couch beside him. "I hope it's not *all* I have to look forward to." He leaned forward, but stopped just short of kissing her. If she wanted him, she'd have to move to kiss him. If she didn't want him—well, he'd rather she not smash his head in.

She took her time deciding. At least, it seemed so to him. He didn't dare move or breathe. He barely dared to blink. And then finally she closed the distance between them, her warm lips brushing over his. She was iron covered in silk, the strength of her always there and shielding her inner softness. He knew she could be soft, and he felt it now in her kiss, in the silkiness of her lips as they trailed over his.

He pulled her into his arms, shifting back so she sat on his lap and he could tangle his fingers in her short hair. His thumbs brushed along her cheeks as he deepened the kiss. And then he did not know if it was the drink or her lips, but he was falling down and down and down into a world of sensation where nothing but her body and her lips and the sound of her breathing existed.

"Kate—" he began.

"Shh. Don't talk. Just kiss me."

He complied, saying what he wanted with his hands and his mouth. *I want you. I love you. I've always loved you.*

He couldn't get enough of her, and when he bent to kiss her neck, she shrugged out of her man's coat. His hands slid up her back, now clothed only in the thin linen shirt. It felt strange to loosen a neckcloth not his own, but he did so easily, then kissed the skin he'd exposed. She was warm, and she smelled clean and pretty—but not feminine. No roses or lilies. She smelled of soap and linen and a hint of mint.

He thought she would stop him when he freed the buttons on her shirt. It would have taken nothing more than a nudge with one of her hands, but she made no move to resist. Instead, she unfastened her cuffs and lifted her hands willingly when he pulled the garment over her head. She straddled him now, her torso bare but for the bindings that pressed her breasts flat. He could see where the linen had been knotted, and he kissed the knot, which elicited a quick inhalation of breath from her.

Using his teeth, he opened the knot, then began the arduous process of unwrapping her. He'd unwound yards of fabric before he caught a glimpse of her skin through the thin linen. And then, as the fabric loosened, her small, round breasts began to take shape, and he could see the outlines of her nipples, pressing against the material. Finally, the last strip of cloth fell away, and she was bare from the waist up. Her skin bore the marks of the tight material, and yet he'd never seen anything more beautiful.

He ran a hand lightly over the angry red marks. "Does it hurt?" he asked.

"No," she said. "I'm used to it. They fade."

He could already see her skin pushing against the indentations, plumping back out and filling in where it had been suppressed. He lifted one breast with his hand and ran his thumb over the distended nipple. She drew in a quick breath and closed her eyes. He repeated the gesture with the other breast, then touched his tongue to her skin. In response, her body slid closer to his, her bottom pressing harder against his erection. He took her into his mouth, suckling gently and teasing the nipple until it swelled and hardened against his tongue.

Her hands fisted in his hair, and her breathing grew faster. "I didn't know that could feel so good," she said on a moan as his mouth moved to her other breast.

She felt good in his arms. She felt as though she belonged there, her skin against his. He couldn't claim that he had much experience with women, but he had always been observant. Kate's responses made it clear what gave her the most pleasure.

"There are other ways to make you feel good," he said against her soft flesh. He allowed his hand to drift to her belly and slide downward. If she'd been wearing a skirt, he might have slid his hands beneath and showed her how he wanted to touch her. But she was wearing trousers, fitted trousers. Seeing her in men's clothing was strange and arousing. His hand dipped to the waistband, and he opened the fall. But of course he would have to remove the trousers to touch her where he wanted. He looked up at her face, seeking permission or compliance.

Slowly, she rose up onto her knees.

Chapter Six

When she rose on her knees, he slid her trousers over her hips, but they would go only so far with her legs spread on either side of him. She would have to climb off and remove her boots, then slip the trousers down and off.

And then what would happen? Would he take her? Was that what she wanted, here on the couch in this room where she'd done all of the dirty work of the Duke of Vauxhall? Maybe Henry was the man who could make her forget all of that for a little while. Maybe with him she could be Kate Dunn once again, not a lord of the underworld.

Henry's hand slid down her bare back and over the swell of her exposed hip. He was so gentle. She hadn't known that men could be gentle. She hadn't known that they could tease and suckle with their mouths. She'd known only that they could take and hurt. Now he pressed his warm mouth against her belly, sending tingles between her legs. His hands slid down and over her bottom, then up the fronts of her thighs. One hand cupped her between the legs, and she could not stop herself from rocking against the pressure he gave, demanding he press harder.

He complied, his eyes, now more blue than gray, on her face. He had beautiful eyes, and she loved how he looked at her, as though he thought she was the most desirable creature he had ever seen. She wasn't. Her hair was short, her face was barely pretty, and her body was too slim and straight. She'd never had trouble passing for a boy, even when she hadn't tried hard to disguise herself.

But she never felt like a boy with Henry. His hands seemed to find her every subtle curve and stroke it. As he touched her, she felt lush and voluptuous, her skin humming with tension and need. His hand moved where she pushed against it, his thumb circling and circling until she inhaled sharply.

He smiled, looking very much like a cat who had a bird in his sights. His thumb moved lazily now, circling that sensitive spot over and over until her legs wobbled and her knees she rested on threatened to buckle. She braced herself, placing her hands on the back of the couch, and he lifted his head and teased her aching nipple with his tongue. She bent to give him better access and gasped when he took it into his mouth. The twin pleasure of his thumb stroking her between the legs and his tongue laving her swollen nipple heightened every sensation until she was no longer certain what she was feeling or how to control it.

She was dimly aware she rocked against him, dimly aware of his free hand holding her up, and she knew he would catch her. He would not let her fall.

The novelty of trusting him—a man—to keep her safe and to give her what she needed was part of the excitement of being with Henry. It had been so long since she'd trusted a man, any man, with any part of herself.

But she surprised herself by trusting Henry—at least for now, in this moment.

And so she could finally let go. When she did, pleasure spiraled upward, hitting her so hard she cried out and jerked. And even that was not enough. The climax ripped through her, making her back arch and her breath catch. Henry held her, his thumb pressing against her, then easing, then pressing again, as though he knew exactly what her body needed.

When the storm passed, when she could breathe again, she looked down at Henry's smoky eyes and didn't know what to say. He'd stripped her armor away, broken her shell, and she felt vulnerable and exposed. It wasn't her nudity that made her feel so. It was the way he seemed to look at her and see *her*, Kate Dunn.

No one had seen Kate Dunn in a long, long time. Not even Kate herself.

"Henry," she said, her voice low and husky. "I don't know what to do now. I don't know what to say."

"Shh," he said with a smile. "Don't talk. Just kiss me."

She knew her own words, and she was glad of them. She bent and kissed him, pressing her body against the heat of him, the wool of his coat scratching her tender breasts. She wanted the coat gone. She wanted nothing between them, his skin sliding against her skin. She pushed the coat off his shoulders, and then a short, quick knock sounded on the door.

"Duke."

"Go away," she said, but she knew even as she said it that the moment was broken.

"We have a problem," Red said from the other side of the door.

There was always a problem. She looked at Henry, and he gave her a rueful smile then handed her the shirt she'd been wearing. "Give me a minute," she told Red.

She disentangled herself from Henry, stood, and fastened her trousers. Not bothering with the bindings for her breasts, she pulled the shirt over her head and grabbed for her coat. Henry stood as well and straightened his own clothing, an easier job since his hadn't been removed.

"I should go," he said. "It's late."

She did not want him to go, but asking him to stay was an even worse idea. They should end this now. They would do their jobs tomorrow and say good-bye. She couldn't afford to develop feelings for him. A voice inside warned her it was too late for that, but she pushed it down.

"Will you be safe on the journey home?" she asked.

He frowned at her. "I don't need you to take care of me."

"I wasn't—" she started. "The gin…"

"My head is clear now," he interrupted. "You have business. I'll see you in the morning, Kate." He bent and kissed her hand, the gesture so far from what she'd expected that she didn't even pull her hand back when he released it. Instead, she stared at her hand for a long moment even after he'd left the room.

It wasn't until Red stomped in that she lowered it and remembered she wasn't a lady.

***

Vauxhall Gardens was lit like a mansion in Mayfair. Kate had never seen it so bright. Every lamp was ablaze, and additional men walked about with torches to light the way of the guests entering. The men and women were brightly dressed, their yellows and oranges contrasting sharply with Kate's sober black coat and black trousers.

"I thought we told him to run out of oil for the lamps," Red said under his breath. He was at Kate's side as they walked past the Grove, where an orchestra played for a small audience.

"We did." Kate was seething, annoyed at the lights and feeling exposed. "He said it was taken care of." She shouldn't have trusted him. She should have sent Scrugs or Davey with him to make sure everything was done as she'd asked.

"Let's hope he got rid of the constables," Red muttered.

Kate was not feeling hopeful. She'd known Henry couldn't call off the Bow Street Runners. They'd be in the gardens until the whole of the prince's celebrations were over, but they'd prepared for a half-dozen Runners. She was not prepared for a score of constables too.

"Let's head toward the dark walks," Red said.

"It appears all we have to do is follow the crowd." Kate nodded at the line of men making their way toward the darkest corner of the gardens. The bare-knuckle fight between Storm aka Emperor and King was the worst-kept secret in London at the moment, and Kate wouldn't have had it any other way. The more people paying to walk through the doors, the better. Others would take home the lion's share of the spectators' fees, but Kate and her gang were handling the betting. That was where the real blunt was. No matter who won, the Duke of Vauxhall would make a pretty profit.

And then Kate and her gang would disappear for the rest of the prince's celebrations. She would lie low until all the fuss was over and then go back to running the regular rackets.

In her head, she could hear the echoes of Henry's warning that her reign as the Duke of Vauxhall couldn't continue forever. In the end, everyone was betrayed. She could only hope that when her end came, it would be swift and painless.

That was all she'd allow herself to hope. Henry might like to delude himself that there was more out there for her, but she knew the truth. This life was all she had. She'd known from childhood that her life would be hard and short. She just hadn't expected to wish it could have been different.

Kate was pleased to note that the lamps were fewer and farther between as they neared the dark walks. A few had even been extinguished, and she thought she could thank her cubs for that work. She was about to ask who Red had assigned to keep watch on this area when he touched her arm in warning. Kate saw the man in the shadows a moment before he stepped out. The warning also gave her time to recognize him, which saved his life. Her hand had gone to the knife at her waist, but now she sheathed it again.

"Bexley," she said. "Nice of you to show your face. We can see it so clearly in all the light."

He frowned but didn't offer an apology. Instead, he stepped back into the shadows. "We need to talk."

Without waiting for her to follow, he started down a dirt path hidden by the bushes. She knew the path well. She was one of the people who'd made it.

"Do you want me to kill him, or do you want the pleasure, Duke?" Red asked, staring after Henry.

"That pleasure is solely mine," she promised. "But let's hear what he has to say first." The hair on the back of her neck prickled, and that was always a bad sign.

Kate and Red followed Henry along the path until they came to an old stone bench, long covered by moss and beginning to crumble. At one time, this section of the gardens must have been open, but it had been forgotten, the trees and bushes around it allowed to grow to conceal it. That suited Kate's purposes very well.

"What do you think you're doing?" Kate said before Henry could try to dominate the discussion. "We were to meet inside the tent. The fight starts in less than an hour."

"We have a problem."

"You're the problem," Red told him.

"No, the Prince Regent is the problem," Henry said.

Kate folded her arms over her chest. "Explain."

"He's here—well, I don't know if he's here yet, but he's coming."

"You said he didn't plan to attend again until the concert and fireworks," Red hissed.

"That was what he said, but he obviously changed his mind. Everyone in Town is talking about this fight. The prince doesn't want to miss it."

Kate put her hand to her forehead in a vain attempt to ward off the megrim she knew was coming. The last thing she needed was the Prince Regent at her prizefight. "And this is why all the lamps are lit?" she asked.

"I had the oil moved so the lamplighters would run out, but when the staff from Prinny's household arrived, they sent for more."

Kate gritted her teeth. "What about the constables?"

"They won't be here tonight, but the prince will have his royal guard with him."

Kate blew out a breath. "That's fine. They'll be here to protect the prince. They won't bother with the rest."

"But you can't still plan to steal the ring," Red asked.

"Why not?"

"What ring?" That was from Henry. Kate wanted to curse.

She ignored the question. "Why not?"

"Because now you have more than the Bow Street Runners and Devonshire's men to contend with. You have Prinny's royal guard as well."

"Devonshire? What the devil?"

Kate kept her gaze on Red. "Which might actually work to our advantage," Kate said.

"Our advantage?" Henry protested. "My tasks for tonight were to eliminate as many constables as I could and rid the gardens of the oil for the lamps. I don't want any part in the rest of it. I bloody well knew there was more to this than the betting, and I don't want to know what else you're planning."

"Then pretend you didn't hear it."

"I wish to hell and back I hadn't, but I'm putting it together now. Devonshire is offering a ring to the winner of the fight, and you think you can steal it. But Devonshire won't hand it over. It will be guarded. And with all the other complications, stealing it is nigh impossible."

"It will certainly be a challenge," she said. And honestly, she had no other choice. This was it. Her last score.

"You'll make a fortune from the betting. Take that and walk away," Henry suggested.

Kate shook her head. "You know I can't do that."

Henry closed his eyes. "I bloody well knew you would say that."

***

Henry followed Kate and Red back to an enormous tent that had been erected deep along one of the dark walks. It was the sort of tent generals might use to confer with staff or within which a sheikh might house his harem. The crowds were spilling out of the flap now, and it was obvious that, despite the size of the tent, not everyone would be able to fit inside. He wasn't certain if the record attendance would help Kate or hurt her.

He didn't know whether he wanted her to be helped or hurt.

Henry didn't condone theft, and he didn't want to be a part of it. It would have made his life so much easier if Kate had been willing to walk away from the theft of the ring. Then she would have been safe—well, safer. But he'd known she never would. Her gang knew she planned to steal the ring, and if she didn't risk it now, she would lose face in their eyes. She couldn't afford that. She had the sort of power that relied upon blunt, violence, and risk. If her gang wasn't in awe of her, afraid of her, or paid well by her, they'd defect to another leader.

She'd said she'd steal the ring. Either she stole it, or she lost everything.

But if she stole the ring, he would lose her.

Henry supposed he would have lost her no matter what, but there had been a moment the night before when he'd hoped they might have a future. Kissing her again had been better than the first time. And touching her, feeling her naked skin beneath his hands, watching her climax—those experiences had been like nothing he could have imagined.

He wanted her again. Even now, he had the urge to touch her, to put a hand on her shoulder or the small of her back. She would cut it off before she allowed his hand on her, though. She was every inch the Duke of Vauxhall at the moment. She moved, spoke, and oozed authority. She didn't have to push past the crowds to gain entrance to the tent. Even if most of the crowd had no idea she was the notorious Duke of Vauxhall, they knew she was someone menacing. The men parted for her without a word of protest, and when she entered the tent, voices hushed.

She didn't pause, but went straight to her gang, who were working the room, collecting bets. Henry followed, glancing around the dark space. The only light was on the ring drawn in the center. Stools for the fighters sat at opposite sides, and Henry recognized Godrick Gunnery standing near his protégé. He rolled his neck and then seemed to nod slightly when the Duke of Vauxhall looked at him.

Scrugs approached Kate immediately. "Duke, we can't fit too many more. Davey and Flasher went to see if there is a way to open up one side. Maybe a few more can sit over there."

"And the betting?" she asked, her voice low. Henry supposed it might sound masculine to someone who didn't know her, but nothing about her appearance would ever seem masculine to him again.

"We're collecting the wagers now," he answered.

"Send some men outside to collect from those who can't get a seat. Even if they don't see the fight, they can still wager."

"Yes, Duke." Scrugs moved away just as a trio of men moved in.

"Runners," Red hissed.

Henry didn't know the men and didn't have any experience with Runners, but now that he knew who they were, he could have picked them out. They exuded the same sort of authority Kate carried.

"Duke," one of the Runners said with a mocking bow. He had a black mustache that looked as though it had been oiled regularly. "We had a feeling you might make an appearance."

"Half of London has made an appearance," Kate said, looking pointedly around the room. "I wouldn't want to miss it."

"Looks like your boys are taking wagers. Has gambling on prizefights at Vauxhall Gardens been sanctioned by the Crown?" the mustached Runner asked.

"Why don't you ask the Prince Regent?" she answered smoothly. "He's wagering twenty pounds on King."

Henry could barely keep his mouth from dropping open. She was lying. He knew she was lying because she hadn't even known the prince was coming, couldn't know whether he would actually attend or not. He certainly hadn't given her any blunt for a wager. But she'd spoken so convincingly that Henry could almost believe she had been chatting with the prince a few moments before entering. The Runners looked skeptical.

The head Runner nodded. "I'll be sure to ask him, Duke. And if I find out differently, we'll come looking for you."

"I'm not a hard man to find." She walked away from the Runners and toward the seats reserved for the Duke of Devonshire. Henry had seen the duke standing near them, and since they were padded and ornamented with gold, he assumed they'd been brought from one of the ducal residences so the man would not have to place his pampered arse on a hard surface.

"Should we offer them a bribe?" Red asked as they walked.

Kate shook her head. "Unfortunately, not all of the Runners are on the take. Those three can't be bought. Keep an eye on them."

"Yes, Duke." And then Red was gone.

Henry moved beside Kate, and she said, almost conversationally, "Introduce me to your friend, won't you?"

He raised his brows. "The Duke of Devonshire is not my friend. We barely know each other."

"That's good enough. Introduce me. I want to see the ring."

Henry clenched his fists. "I told you I don't want to be part of this," he said under his breath.

"Too late for that, Henry." She stopped a few feet before the circle of sycophants surrounding Devonshire.

Devonshire paused in his conversation, his questioning gaze traveling from her to Henry.

"Duke," Henry said genially. Devonshire's friends called him Hart, but as Henry had said, he was not one of Devonshire's friends. "Allow me to introduce you to an…acquaintance of mine." He'd purposefully paused, as though reluctant to call Kate an acquaintance. As though his association with the crime lord was forced. "The Duke of Vauxhall."

The duke's gaze lowered to Kate briefly. "Sir."

Kate bowed with gentlemanly courtesy. She would have made a wonderful actress if she hadn't been a crime lord. "Your Grace. Thank you for offering the prize to the winner of the match tonight. I've heard the ring is quite spectacular."

The duke didn't answer, but he inclined his head toward a footman in the Devonshire livery. The man held a silver tray in the center of which was an ornate wooden box that would have fit snugly in a man's palm. He approached and, with a gloved hand, opened the lid. Henry had seen many riches, but even his eyes widened at the sight of the ring. It was gold and sparkled with diamonds. The band was thick and masculine and in the center of the ring, surrounded by diamonds, was a large square-cut stone.

"Perfect," Kate said, managing to look almost disinterested. "A fine prize." She bowed and then moved away. Henry bowed as well and followed. He looked back and saw the footman had returned to his place, holding the tray with the box, once again closed, but in full view.

"You seem unimpressed," he said, keeping his voice low.

"No reason to appear too interested." She steered them to the seats that had been reserved for her, to the left of the duke and in the front. There were two seats, and both were occupied by gang members who stood and moved aside when she approached. "Sit back down," she told them. "I won't be sitting much." To Henry, she said, "You won't be sitting at all. I want you far away when I take the ring."

"You don't have to do this. You could come with me—"

She waved a hand, cutting him off. "We both know I can't accept that offer, and you don't even have the right to make it. I wish we were alone, so I could say good-bye. But this will have to do." She made him a formal bow, such as one might give a mere acquaintance.

Henry didn't know why he should feel as though he'd been slapped. This was what they had planned. This was the way it was supposed to happen. He was free now. He could walk away, and he'd never have to see the Duke of Vauxhall again. The prince's celebrations would go on as planned, and he could take all the credit and glory for both the grandeur and the economy.

It was what he'd always wanted, wasn't it? It was the safest course.

Henry made his way out of the tent, feeling safer than he had in days.

And hating it.

Chapter Seven

When Henry was gone, Kate squared her shoulders and went to work. There was no point in thinking about Henry any longer. She'd told him to leave, and he had. That was what she'd wanted. That was what they'd agreed upon. The traps were set, and all that was left was for her to do her part.

She couldn't afford distractions right now.

Kate paced the area between her seats and that of the duke, trying to look like a man with a lot on his mind and much responsibility. She was all of that as her cubs reported to her, and she had to make decisions, such as when to close the flaps of the tent and not allow any more spectators inside. All the time, she kept the box with the ring in the periphery of her vision. She was aware of the number of times it was opened and who held it and when it was passed to someone else.

She'd picked pockets so often she could have done it in her sleep. Usually, it thrilled her, made her blood race in her veins. Tonight, she just wanted it done. She didn't know why. Henry would not be waiting for her at the end. This was it. This was all she had in her life now.

Finally, the fight was about to begin. She had delayed the start to give the Prince Regent more time to arrive, but if she delayed too long, the spectators, who had been drinking and were now tightly packed into the stuffy room, would begin fighting amongst themselves. Women had not been allowed to attend the fight, but some had ignored the rule and were inside anyway. A fight over a woman would be all she needed.

Kate signaled to Gentleman Jackson. As the best-known fighter in England, he'd been asked to officiate, and he would determine the winner if neither pugilist was knocked unconscious. Now, Jackson stood in the middle of the ring and introduced the two competitors. Each man received loud cheers when his name was announced.

Kate continued pacing.

Next, the Duke of Devonshire was singled out, and the box with the ring was opened and displayed for all to see. The crowd reacted with the expected admiration. Finally, Jackson was ready to begin the fight, but Kate had caught a sign from one of the cubs near the entry flap. She smiled. She'd needed a distraction and thought she would have to satisfy herself with the first punches of the fight. But this would be even better. She nodded to the cub, then held up a hand to stay Jackson's next words.

She didn't need to speak, because the commotion the prince made as he entered the tent was more than sufficient to announce his arrival. He was fat, and the room was too full, and he struggled to make his way through the throngs. One of her cubs led his royal guard to her seats, and Kate made a show of bowing as though offering them to the prince. She didn't speak, and the prince didn't thank her. He merely took the seats and waved a scented handkerchief in front of his face. Kate moved out of the prince's way to accommodate his retinue, which meant she was pushed closer to the Duke of Devonshire's staff. Closer to the silver tray with the ring box in the center. It took only a moment, a moment when all attention was on the prince and then on Jackson, and the ring was hers.

She hadn't become the Duke of Vauxhall simply because she was clever. She was also the best thief in London.

She pocketed the ring and nodded to Red. The two of them headed for the exit. No one paid them any attention. All eyes were on the men, stripped to the waist, battling in the center of the room. Kate was small, and it was easy for her to slip through the crowds. In a matter of minutes, she was outside and walking quickly away from the tent.

Red was right behind her. "That went better than I thought it would," he said.

Kate didn't reply. As far as she was concerned, the game was far from over. If she'd been on the streets of London, this would have been the moment when her hand was still in the mark's pocket, and her wrist could be snatched at any second. And then, as though her thought had made it real, she heard an uproar from the tent that had nothing to do with a well-thrown punch.

"Here we go," she told Red. "The fun is starting."

"I'm too old for fun." But he took off in one direction, and she in the other, as the Runners poured out of the tent and dodged after them.

Kate knew she had Henry to thank for the fact that she had only Runners to contend with and not any constables. Still, she cursed his name when three of them arrowed straight for her. She'd hoped more of them would go for Red, as he was a larger target, but she supposed she could handle three—if everything had been prepared correctly.

Kate ran in the direction she'd walked countless times over the past few days. She knew the way even in the dark, which was a good thing, as her cubs had managed to extinguish or break all of the lamps in this section. She'd have to remember to give them a reward. While she'd been busy inside the tent, they'd been working out here. She ran straight for the first trap, jumping nimbly over a pile of leaves. She heard the Runners right behind her, then heard the telltale cry as the ground under the leaves gave way.

She dared a look over her shoulder, then blew out an exasperated breath as she spotted two Runners on the side of the pit. Only one had fallen in. The other two had been either too deft or far enough back to avoid the trap. She might have hoped the Runners would stay long enough with their fallen comrade for her to escape, but they left him in the pit and raced after her.

Kate shifted direction and moved toward the second trap. This one was trickier, because she had to run close to a tree, and in the dark, all the trees looked alike. Not to mention, the Runners would be averse to moving too close to trees because they wouldn't want to be struck by low-hanging branches. And they'd be alert for traps now.

Kate would have to run faster to counter their new cautiousness. She kicked up her speed until the muscles in her calves felt tight and her chest burned. At this speed, it was difficult to see which tree she needed, and she swore when she realized she'd passed it. She'd have to keep running then double back. She lost time this way, but it couldn't be helped.

Red wasn't wrong when he'd said he was too old for this sort of thing. Kate might have been barely six and twenty, but she was tired. Tired of running. Tired of the chase and the near misses. She'd never had much to lose before if she'd been caught. Her life hadn't meant anything.

But since she'd met Henry, she'd begun to look forward to seeing him. She'd imagined kissing him again. She'd anticipated his company.

She'd lost him too now, and somehow that made all the rest seem meaningless.

Kate doubled back, careful not to accidentally run straight into the Runners' arms, and made straight for the tree. Slowing so her pursuers would be right behind her, she veered off at the very last second, not certain she would evade the trap herself until she didn't feel the net closing around her. She stumbled on, dodging the other trees just as she heard the whoosh of the net and the yells of the Runners.

Kate circled a tree and leaned against the trunk to catch her breath. She gulped in air, then peered around the trunk.

And swore.

One Runner was standing under the net, looking up at his partner. "Damn it!" she muttered. She was out of traps. Red's traps might have been more efficient than hers, but if she led the Runner toward the path Red had taken and Red hadn't yet evaded all of his pursuers, she could put them both in danger.

The last Runner turned to look in her direction, and she saw it was the mustachioed man. Of course it had to be him. He was the smartest of the lot, and probably the strongest. She'd be no match against him in a hand-to-hand fight. She'd have to lose him.

She started running again, wishing her legs were longer, or that she had better-fitting boots. She supposed the situation could have been worse than simply crashing through a garden in the dark. She could have been crashing through a garden in the dark while wearing skirts and slippers.

She led the Runner in circles several times, but finally it became clear he was catching up to her. He was probably in better physical shape than she and used to chasing criminals. That was, after all, why he was called a Runner. She had little choice but to sprint toward her exit. Maybe she could run fast enough to leave Vauxhall behind. There were many places she could hide along the road. She could even jump on a carriage or cart and hide there.

Kate left the formerly booby-trapped section of the gardens behind and started for the back of Vauxhall. She had hidden burrows along the back wall and could scuttle under in a few moments. She'd just have to hope she'd be faster than he was, or he'd grab her ankle and pull her right back in.

That hope was quickly erased, because as soon as the foliage thinned, he increased his speed. She could all but feel his breath on the back of her neck.

"I have you, Duke!" he panted.

"Not yet," she said and tried to run faster.

She passed a tree, her eyes on the wall beyond—the wall she would never be able to burrow under without him catching her. Too late, she saw the shadow behind the tree. She threw up her arms to ward off the attack and closed her eyes.

But when she heard the thud, she didn't feel any pain.

Kate opened her eyes and saw Henry standing on the other side of the tree. The Runner lay at his feet.

***

Henry grabbed Kate's arms. "Are you hurt?" he asked, looking into her eyes. Her face was red with exertion and her eyes wild. She looked from him to the Runner and back again.

"What are you doing?" she asked. "You're supposed to be away from here."

He released her. "I suppose it's too much to expect a *thank you*."

"I suppose it's too much to expect you to do what I tell you." Her hands went to her hips and she gulped in air.

"I don't work for you. I don't follow your orders."

She stared at him, her thoughts unreadable under her trained expression. Then, to his surprise, she smiled. "No, you don't work for me, do you?" She looked down at the Runner again. "What did you do to him?"

Henry shrugged and lifted a tree branch. "He should be unconscious for a little while."

"Good." She nodded quickly. "That gives me time."

Henry looked at the wall. He'd given her time to escape now. That hadn't been his plan. He'd planned to wait for her and give her a proper good-bye, but when he'd heard her coming and heard the footsteps behind her, he'd known she wasn't alone. That was when he'd lifted the branch.

"Is it enough time for a last kiss?" he asked. "We didn't say a proper farewell."

"No," Kate said. "There's not time for that."

Henry nodded coldly. It was probably better this way. If he kissed her again, he'd only want more and more, and he already wanted her too much.

"Help me take this coat off," Kate said.

Henry stared at her.

"The coat, Henry. Hurry."

He took one of the sleeves, and she yanked her arm out. "I have a dress hidden in those shrubs," she told him.

She had planned for everything, it seemed.

She held out her hand for the coat, but instead of taking it, she reached inside. When her hand was free, she opened it. Gold and diamonds glittered on her palm.

"You got it."

She smiled. "Of course I did."

Then she leaned down, opened the Runner's hand, and placed the ring inside, closing his fist around it.

Henry watched her with growing horror. "What are you doing?"

She looked up at him. "Does your offer still stand?"

"My offer?"

"Do you still want me?"

"Yes." He didn't have to think about it. He wanted her, no matter the price.

"I'm not doing you any favors. If we marry, you'll regret it. We'll both regret it."

Henry pulled her into his arms. "Never. You're not the only one who can make plans, you know."

"You have a plan?"

"If you can get us out of Vauxhall Gardens, I can take care of our future."

"Done." She started for the wall, stripping off her shirt and her bindings as she went. It amazed Henry how quickly she worked and how unconcerned she might be that she might be seen, half naked. She bent and retrieved a small satchel, then pulled out a dress. She yanked it over her head and then reached under the skirts to unfasten her trousers and remove them.

She was pinning the bodice into place when Henry could finally believe she was serious. She was giving up her life as the Duke of Vauxhall. She'd not be able to go back when the Runner awoke with the ring. Even her own gang wouldn't stand behind her once they learned she'd failed to pinch the goods.

"Are you certain?" Henry asked. He looked pointedly back at the Runner.

Kate took his hands. "No looking back. No regrets."

"Why?"

She put a finger to his mouth. "Ask me again when we're away from here. For now, this is why." And she lifted her finger and pressed her lips to his.

***

Back at The Griffin and the Unicorn, Kate shoved the few possessions she didn't want to lose into her satchel. There wasn't much. She didn't want anything to remind her of her life as the Duke of Vauxhall. Instead, she took personal items—a brush, clothing, and a miniature of her parents.

The gang hadn't returned yet, and the inn was empty except for the servants preparing for the return of the guests who had gone to Vauxhall for the night. "If we leave now, we'll have a good start on them," she said. "But we can't go to your house. They'll look for me there."

Henry nodded as though he knew this. "I didn't intend to go there."

"Then where did you intend?"

"The docks." He pulled a paper from his waistcoat. "We're leaving England."

She raised her brows. "This is your plan? Flee the country?"

"No one will find you if you're not in England to be found."

She couldn't argue with him. "And you have all the papers?"

"I arranged everything days ago. I kept hoping I might be able to convince you."

"But leave England and your title...everything?"

"We'll come back," he promised.

Kate frowned. "How can we?"

Henry put his hands on her shoulders. "Do you trust me, Kate?"

She didn't answer for a long, long time. She'd never trusted anyone. She'd never dared. But hadn't she already trusted Henry when she'd put the ring in the Runner's hand?

"Yes," she finally said, looking up at him. "I trust you."

He kissed her. "Then let's go."

Chapter Eight

Kate stood at the porthole and stared out at the open ocean. Henry had been on ships before, but he didn't think she had. She'd been stumbling around for the last few hours, trying to get her sea legs, and now that they were inside the luxurious guest cabin he'd arranged, she had spent the better part of an hour staring at the ocean.

"What do you see?" he asked, coming up behind her.

"Water," she answered. "A lot of water. I don't like it."

"We'll be on land again soon."

She nodded and continued staring out at the ocean.

"Do you regret leaving?" he asked finally. "I cannot turn the ship around, but if you want to go back, I will find a way to take you back."

Slowly, she turned to him. Her hand came up to cup his cheek. "I don't deserve you, Henry."

His chest tightened. "Of course you do."

"I don't, but that has never stopped me from taking what I want. And I realized tonight that I want you."

He could breathe again, but he felt a hitch. "You just realized that tonight?"

She gave him an enthusiastic hug, an action he hadn't expected. The force of her embrace caused him to stumble back, and the two of them landed on the berth, Kate sprawled on top of him. Henry tried to sit, but Kate pushed him back down. "I like you where you are, Henry Selkirk."

"I rather like it too."

"Good. Then listen to what I have to say, because I won't say it again. I'm not the sort of chit who fans her face with a handkerchief and waxes poetical about love."

He knew that all too well. "I like you just fine exactly the way you are. Well, assuming you don't acquire another iron rod."

Her fingers twined with his. "You are safe with me, Henry." She bent and kissed his lips. "Always and forever," she whispered.

He raised his brows. This was indeed a side of her he hadn't expected.

"Do you know what I realized tonight?" she asked.

"I cannot imagine."

She began to unfasten her bodice. "Red said he was too old to run away from Bow Street Runners. I realized I'm too old to do it anymore too. I'm too old and too tired. I know I'm not elderly, but I've spent a lifetime ducking and dodging. I did it to survive, and I did it because it made my blood race. But it doesn't make my blood race anymore, Henry. When you walked out of that tent, I wanted to chase after you. I didn't want to lose you, because you, Henry—*you* make my blood race."

"I know the feeling," he said, looking up at her as she slid the dress off her shoulders, revealing her bare breasts.

"I never cared about losing anyone before. It was part of the cost of business. But I didn't want to lose you, Henry. I couldn't lose you, and I couldn't keep you and remain the Duke of Vauxhall." She untied his neckcloth and flung it on the floor and began to unfasten his shirt buttons. "And that was a perfectly acceptable trade, because here's a secret, Henry." She pulled him up, pushed his coat off and gathered his shirt over his head. Then her hands rested on his bare shoulders, and she looked directly in his eyes. "I hated being the Duke of Vauxhall."

"You hated it?" His hands slid up her bare back, and he pulled her close. He wanted to feel her skin touch his.

"I hated always watching my back. I hated never trusting anyone. I hated expecting that at any moment someone would try to kill me."

He slid his hands into her skirts and pushed the dress over her hips. "It makes life less pleasurable," he said.

"Yes," she murmured against his neck as she moved her body so he could help her wiggle out of the dress. "I never thought I would see you again, and when I did, I remembered what my life had been. I remembered what it felt like to trust and to love." She looked up at him. "I love you, Henry. I've always loved you."

He dropped her dress on the floor, and she straddled him, naked.

"And I trust you," she said. "I've always trusted you."

"You can always trust me," he said. "I have a plan, and it's really quite simple. We'll go to France and—"

She kissed him, long and deep, and when she pulled away, he'd forgotten what he'd been saying.

"Why don't we talk about the plan later?" she said, and she pushed him back on the berth and kissed him again.

He let her have her way, let her tease him with her lips and her hands, until he thought he would go mad. Then he flipped her over and had his way, exploring her body and reveling in every little moan and sigh. She was the Kate he'd always loved, and she was also the woman he'd fallen in love with.

And when she took him in, when she opened herself to him, and the last of her defenses fell away, he fell in love with her all over again.

Later, he dozed while she stroked his hair back from his head. "Don't you ever sleep?" he murmured.

"Sleeping is a hazard if you're a crime lord."

"I see." He vowed one day she would feel safe again.

"You said something earlier about a plan. I believe you were rudely interrupted."

"Pleasantly interrupted." He faced her and propped his chin on his hand. "Would you like to know my plan now?"

"Please."

"You may not know that the Viscounts Bexley have properties in France and Austria. When we reach France, I will send notices back to England that I was called to one of my Continental estates on urgent business."

"And that will appease the prince?"

"Oh, the prince will only be too happy to have me out of the way and no longer holding the purse strings. You and I will travel the Continent—"

"By land, I hope."

"Yes, by land. And you will adopt a new identity. You can be anyone you want, though for my purposes it would be best if you choose to become a noblewoman."

She smiled. "A noblewoman? I like that."

"I thought you might. Then we grow your hair out, have a new wardrobe made for you, and perhaps feed you a bit more."

"Are you saying I'm too thin?"

"I am saying you could do with a few more pounds if we are to change your appearance."

"And then, when we return, I look different and you call me a different name, and no one ever knows I was once the Duke of Vauxhall."

"That's it. Except for one small point."

"What's that?"

"You must also return as my wife."

"Your wife?"

"You'd be a viscountess."

She frowned. "I'd probably hate that."

"Probably as much as I hate being a viscount."

She smiled. "We could hate it together."

"We could use our influence to help the poor."

She waved a hand. "We could use our influence to annoy all those nobs with their noses in the air."

He laughed. "That too." He took her hand and kissed her palm. "What do you say, Kate?" Henry held his breath. For a man who was cautious to a fault, he felt as though he was laying himself open, not only to rejection but to the danger of exposure and ridicule.

And it was all worth it to have her by his side.

Kate squeezed his hand. "I say yes."

"You won't regret it."

"Neither will you," she promised.

***

But Henry did have one regret in the end. Months later, he learned that after he'd left England, not only had the prince exceeded his budget for the celebrations at Vauxhall, but he'd also spent a fortune that had even the most liberal of his financial counselors shaking their heads and cursing the foreign holdings of Viscount Bexley.

Henry would have liked to have been the man who'd taken the prince and his lavish spending in hand, but one could not have everything. And Henry had the most important thing of all.

His darling.

His love.

His duke.

Acknowledgments

This novella originally appeared in an anthology titled *The Dukes of Vauxhall*, along with related novellas by Theresa Romain, Christi Caldwell, and Vanessa Kelly. Thanks to Vanessa, Christi, and Theresa for being so much fun to work with and for all your help with this novella.

I also want to acknowledge Joyce Lamb for her stellar copyediting and Sarah Rosenbarker, who proofed the manuscript. Any and all mistakes are my own, but readers would be writing me more letters if not for these consummate professionals.

About Shana Galen

Shana Galen is a three-time Rita Award nominee and the bestselling author of passionate Regency romps, including the RT Reviewers' Choice *The Making of a Gentleman*. Kirkus says of her books, "The road to happily-ever-after is intense, conflicted, suspenseful and fun," and *RT Book Reviews* calls her books "lighthearted yet poignant, humorous yet touching." She taught English at the middle and high school level off and on for eleven years. Most of those years were spent working in Houston's inner city. Now she writes full time. She's happily married and has a daughter who is most definitely a romance heroine in the making.

Wonder what Shana has coming next? Join Shana's mailing list, and be the first to receive information on sales and new releases. Shana never spams or sells readers' information.

Books by Shana Galen

Dive into one of Shana's many other titles…

Regency Spies
While You Were Spying
When Dashing Met Danger
Pride and Petticoats

Misadventures in Matrimony
No Man's Bride
Good Groom Hunting
Blackthorne's Bride
The Pirate Takes a Bride

Sons of the Revolution
The Making of a Duchess
The Making of a Gentleman
The Rogue Pirate's Bride

Jewels of the Ton
If You Give a Duke a Diamond
If You Give a Rake a Ruby
Sapphires are an Earl's Best Friend

Lord and Lady Spy
Lord and Lady Spy

The Spy Wore Blue (novella)
True Spies
Love and Let Spy
All I Want for Christmas is Blue (novella)
The Spy Beneath the Mistletoe (novella)

Covent Garden Cubs
Viscount of Vice (novella)
Earls Just Want to Have Fun
The Rogue You Know
I Kissed a Rogue

The Survivors
Third Son's a Charm
No Earls Allowed
An Affair with a Spare (coming July 2018)
Unmask Me if You Can (coming November 2018)

The Scarlet Chronicles
Traitor in Her Arms
To Ruin a Gentleman (coming January 2019)
Taken by the Rake (coming February 2019)
To Tempt a Rebel (coming March 2019)

Standalones and Anthologies
The Summer of Wine and Scandal (novella)
A Royal Christmas (duet)
The Dukes of Vauxhall (anthology)
How to Find a Duke in Ten Days (anthology)
A Grosvernor Square Christmas (anthology)

Made in the USA
Coppell, TX
12 August 2022

81401087R00125